WORLD FAMOUS FICTIONS

THE LAST OF THE MOHICANS

By
JAMES FENIMORE COOPER

With Chinese Translation by
WOO KWANG KIEN

THE COMMERCIAL PRESS, LIMITED
SHANGHAI, CHINA
1934

末了的摩希干人

傳　略

　　庫柏(Cooper)生於美國的紐佐爾細(New Jersey)是一七八九至一八五一年間人。他的父親是英國的朋友會中人，他的母親是瑞典人的後裔。他在耶魯(Yale)大學三年，因事出校，這就同好幾個在他之前及在他之後的有名的文學家一樣，都是忽然離開大學的。他入海軍供職四年。後來做田舍翁，頗研究邊境上土人的生活，及殖民地時代的歷史。他遊歷英國，德國，瑞士國，當過法國里昂(Lyons)領事。他死於一八五一年，瀕死時囑咐家裏，不必搜輯材料，爲他作傳。他有三十多種著作，出名的有十種八種小說，尤以今所選譯的『末了的摩希干人』爲最出名。這部小說敘一七五五年英法兩國爭北美洲土地的事，地點在哈得孫(Hudson)河源與附近諸湖之間，以土酋安伽斯及當探子的英國人綽號"鷹眼"的爲主要人物。作者有的頗犯文法的規；馬可特威英(Mark Twain)說撰小說有撰小說的規則，庫柏卻什犯其八九。魯安波里教授說，可惜庫柏到了第三年就出學——這就好像是說耶魯或其他大學曾幫助過一個有天才的人撰小說！其實他的小說以材料勝，他狀物敍事又最能引人入勝，令人不忍釋手。他的小說在歐洲三十處大城市出版，幾乎與司各脫(Scott)及擺倫(Byron)齊名。巴爾札克(Balzac)也是一個好犯撰小說規則的人，卻恭維庫柏，說他的閎壯肅穆只有司各脫能及，可謂推崇到極點了。民國二十二年癸酉處暑日伍光建記。

末 了 的 摩 希 干 人
THE LAST OF THE MOHICANS

THE LAST OF THE MOHICANS

CHAPTER XXI

"If you find a man there, he shall die a flea's death."
—THE MERRY WIVES OF WINDSOR.

The party had landed on the border of a region that is, even to this day, less known to the inhabitants of the States, than the deserts of Arabia, or the steppes of Tartary. It was the sterile and rugged district which separates the tributaries of Champlain from those of the Hudson, the Mohawk, and the St. Lawrence. Since the period of our tale the active spirit of the country has surrounded it with a belt of rich and thriving settlements, though none but the hunter or the savage is ever known even now to penetrate its wild recesses.

As Hawkeye and the Mohicans had, however, often traversed the mountains and valleys of this vast wilderness, they did not hesitate to plunge into its depths, with the freedom of men accustomed to its privations[1] and difficulties. For many hours the travellers toiled on their laborious way, guided by a star, or following the direction of some water-course, until the scout called a halt and holding a short consultation with the Indians, they lighted their fire, and made the usual preparations to pass the remainder of the night where they then were.

[1] privations 窮乏; 缺乏.

4

末了的摩希干人

第二十一回　追蹤

〔英法兩國爭北美土地，各利用土酋爲助；法軍利用胡倫人 (Hurons) 的酋長馬伽 (Magua)，英軍有安伽斯(Uncas 卽所謂末了一個摩希干人 Mohicans)相助。英軍礮台被圍，軍長不派兵來援，台官孟洛(Munro)力盡約降，挈兩女逃避，被馬伽狙擊，馬伽捉兩女，英軍探子綽號鷹眼 Hawk-eye 與安伽斯等追尋兩女下落——譯者註。〕

　　這羣人到了一個地方的邊界，現在美國的居民還不甚曉得這個地方，不如他們曉得阿剌伯的沙漠或韃靼利的高原那樣清楚。這是一片不毛不平的地方，分開查木披倫河 (Champlain) 及哈特生河 (Hudson)，摩覆克河 (Mohawk) 及聖羅倫斯河 (St. Lawrence) 各支流。在我們這篇故事之後，地方的活動精神建設許多富而發達的僑居地，包圍這塊地方，但是到了現在，亦只有獵人或土人，深入這塊深密的野地。

　　因爲鷹眼及摩希干人屢次在這片大野地的高山及深谷走過，他們毫不遲疑的深入內地，他們受慣窮困艱難的痛苦，隨便就深入。這些旅行人很辛苦的走了幾點鐘難走的路，或靠一顆星作嚮導，或跟着溪流的方向走，等到後來探子吩咐暫停，同印度人商量片時，打火造飯，預備在他們這時候所在的地方過夜。

THE LAST OF THE MOHICANS

Imitating the example, and emulating[1] the confidence of their more experienced associates, Munro and Duncan slept without fear, if not without uneasiness. The dews were suffered to exhale, and the sun had dispersed the mists, and was shedding a strong and clear light in the forest, when the travellers resumed their journey.

After proceeding a few miles, the progress of Hawkeye, who led the advance, became more deliberate[2] and watchful. He often stopped to examine the trees; nor did cross a rivulet, without attentively considering the quantity, the velocity, and the color of its waters. Distrusting his own judgment, his appeals to the opinion of Chingachgook were frequent and earnest. During one of these conferences Heyward observed that Uncas stood a patient and silent, though, as he imagined, an interested[3] listener. He was strongly tempted to address the young chief, and demand his opinion of their progress; but the clam and dignified demeanor of the native induced him to believe, that, like himself, the other was wholly dependent on the sagacity and intelligence of the seniors of the party. At last the scout spoke in English, and at once explained the embarrassment of their situation.

"When I found that the home path of the Hurons run north," he said, "it did not need the judgment of many long years to tell that they would follow the valleys, and keep atween the waters of the Hudson and the Horican, until they might strike the springs of the Canada streams, which would lead them into the heart of the country of the Frenchers. Yet here are we, within a short range of

---

1 emulating 爭 勝.　　2 deliberate 費 商 量; 費 事.　　3 interested 注 意; 休 戚 相 關.

末 了 的 摩 希 干 人

　　孟洛及旦肯(Duncan 他是英軍的少佐——譯者註。)學他們的榜樣，又要同他們的更富於閱歷的同伴們的深信不疑爭勝，也就睡下，倘容或覺得不安，卻是毫不害怕的，睡下了。當他們再走路的時候，露水已經蒸化了，太陽也把霧驅散了，放出烈而清朗的光，照在樹林。

　　鷹眼在前頭走，走了不多幾哩，就起首走得慢些，又更留心些。他屢次站着觀察樹木；當他快要過溪的時候，他先要留心察看水有多少，流得快慢，及水的顏色。他不相信自己的判斷，還要屢次鄭重的請教慶伽谷 (Chingach-gook 他是安伽斯的父親——譯者註。) 有一次正在商量的時候，哈華特 (Heyward 卽是旦肯——譯者註。)看見安伽斯很耐煩的又不響的站着，但是據他看來，安伽斯很注意聽他們說話。他很想同這個少年酋長說話，要請教他應該怎樣進步；但是這個土人的鎮靜的及莊厲的態度使他相信，他自己同他一樣，都完全依靠這一羣人裏頭的年紀較長的人們的靈敏及明智，後來探子說英國話，立刻解說他們的爲難境地。

　　他說道，『當我見得胡倫人回家所走的路是向北行，那就用不着有多年閱歷的人說他們應該跟着山谷走，在哈特生河與荷爾力甘之間走，走到他們可以遇着加拿大諸河的支流，這就會引他們入法蘭西人所在的腹地。但是

THE LAST OF THE MOHICANS

the Scaroons, and not a sign of a trail[1] have we crossed! Human natur' is weak, and it is possible we may not have taken the proper scent."

"Heaven protect us from such an error!" exclaimed Duncan. "Let us retrace our steps, and examine as we go, with keener eyes. Has Uncas no counsel to offer in such a strait?"[2]

The young Mohican cast a glance at his father, but maintaining his quiet and reserved mien, he continued silent. Chingachgook had caught the look, and motioning with his hand, he bade him speak. The moment this permission was accorded, the countenance of Uncas changed from its grave composure to a gleam of intelligence and joy. Bounding forward like a deer, he sprang up the side of a little declivity, a few rods in advance, and stood, exultingly, over a spot of fresh earth, that looked as though it had been recently upturned by the passage of some heavy animal. The eyes of the whole party followed the unexpected movement, and read their success in the air of triumph that the youth assumed.

" 'Tis the trail!" exclaimed the scout, advancing to the spot; "the lad is quick of sight and keen of wit for his years."

" 'Tis extraordinary that he should have withheld his knowledge so long," muttered Duncan, at his elbow.

"It would have been more wonderful had he spoken without a bidding. No, no; your young white, who gathers his learning from books and can measure what he knows by the page, may conceit[3] that his knowledge, like his legs,

---

[1] trail 行蹤; 脚跡.　[2] strait 缺乏; 爲難.　[3] conceit 自以爲是; 自傲, 妄自尊大.

8

現在我們離斯卡倫斯（Scaroons）不遠，我們卻並未經過
他們的行蹤！人的聰明原是薄弱的，也許我們不曾走進尋
他們的行蹤所應走的路。』

　　旦肯喊道，『天保護我們，不令我們作這樣的錯事。
我們不如退步，一面走一面用更尖利的眼，細心察看。我
們遇着這樣的爲難，難道安伽斯無策可獻麼？』

　　這個少年摩希干人看看他的父親，但仍保留他的安
靜及緘默態度，接連不開口。慶伽谷看見兒子看他一眼，
動一動他的手，叫他說話。安伽斯一得了這樣的許可，他
的嚴重安詳變作一陣過而不留的聰明及歡樂。他同一隻
鹿一般，跳向前，跳上在前不過幾十碼的一條小斜徑的邊
上，很得意的站在一塊新土上，好像是重大的動物新近才
翻起來的。全隊人的眼睛都跟着這樣出其不意的舉動，一
看那個少年的得意神色，就曉得他們找着行蹤了。

　　探子走到那個地點，喊道，『這是行蹤；他這樣年紀的
孩子，虧他有這樣快的眼光，有這樣利的聰明。』

　　旦肯在他的身邊，喃喃的說道，『他久已曉得了，卻不
肯說出，這是太奇怪了。』

　　探子說道，『假使他未奉命就先說出，那才是更奇怪
呢。不奇，不奇；你們的少年白人，從書本裏頭採取知識，
可以用多少頁書以算有多少知識，可以妄自尊大，說他的

outruns that of his father; but where experience is the master, the scholar is made to know the value of years, and respects them accordingly."

"See!" said Uncas, pointing north and south, at the evident marks of the broad trail on either side of him, "the dark-hair has gone toward the frost."

"Hound never ran on a more beautiful scent," responded the scout, dashing forward, at once, on the indicated route; "we are favored, greatly favored, and can follow with high noses. Ay, here are both your waddling beasts; this Huron travels like a white general. The fellow is stricken with a judgment, and is mad! Look sharp for wheels, Sagamore," he continued, looking back, and laughing in his newly awakened satisfaction; "we shall soon have the fool journeying in a coach, and that with three of the best pair of eyes on the borders in his rear."

The spirits of the scout, and the astonishing success of the chase, in which a circuitous distance of more than forty miles had been passed, did not fail to impart a portion of hope to the whole party. Their advance was rapid; and made with as much confidence as a traveller would proceed along a wide highway. If a rock, or a rivulet, or a bit of earth harder than common, severed the links of the clew they followed, the true eye of the scout recovered them at a distance, and seldom rendered the delay of a single moment necessary. Their progress was much facilitated by the certainty that Magua had found it necessary to journey through the valleys; a circumstance which rendered the general direction of the route sure. Nor had the Huron entirely neglected the arts uniformly practised by the natives when retiring in front of an enemy. False trails and sudden turnings were frequent, wherever a brook

知識，如同他的兩脚勝過他的父親；但是若以閱歷為主，學者要曉得年紀的價值，所以要尊重有年紀的人。』

安伽斯向南北兩方指，指在他兩旁的寬廣行蹤的顯然標記，說道，『看呀！黑髮人向樹林去了。』

探子立刻衝上前，到了所指示的路徑上，答道，『獵狗也找不出更好的蹤跡，我們僥倖，大僥倖，我們能夠抬起頭來跟行蹤走。呀，這裏是你們的兩個搖搖擺擺走得慢的動物；這個胡倫人旅行，同一個白人的軍長一樣。這個人受了裁判了，他是瘋了！』他回頭看，他得了新鮮醒悟的滿意，對酋長說道，『你留心看車輪，我們不久會看見這個傻子坐大車走路，用三個眼光最好的看着後面的邊界。』

探子的高興，追趕所得的令人詫異的成功，又繞路走過四十多哩，不能不給這羣人以一部分的希望。他們進行甚快；他們很果於自信的進行，如同一個旅行人在大路上前進一樣。若有一塊山石，一條溪流，或一塊比尋常更堅硬的土，打斷他們所跟隨的行蹤，探子的準確的眼就在相離不遠地方再找着，很少得要停頓躭擱一會兒的工夫。他們曉得馬伽見得必要走過山谷；這樣的情形就使他們所走的路的大概方向有了定準的；他們的進步就變作容易得多。胡倫人並未整個的忽略土人在仇敵前面退走時所一律習用的詭計。他們往往利用假行蹤及忽然轉灣，遇着

or the formation of the ground rendered them feasible; but his pursuers were rarely deceived, and never failed to detect their error, before they had lost either time or distance on the deceptive track.

By the middle of the afternoon they had passed the Scaroons and were following the route of the declining sun. After descending an eminence to a low bottom, through which a swift stream glided, they suddenly came to a place where the party of Le Renard had made a halt. Extinguished brands were lying around a spring, the offals of a deer were scattered about the place, and the trees bore evident marks of having been browsed by the horses. At a little distance, Heyward discovered, and contemplated with tender emotion, the small bower under which he was fain to believe that Cora and Alice had reposed. But while the earth was trodden, and the footsteps of both men and beasts were so plainly visible around the place, the trail appeared to have suddenly ended.

It was easy to follow the tracks of the Narragansetts, but they seemed only to have wandered without guides, or any other object than the pursuit of food. At length Uncas, who, with his father had endeavored to trace the route of the horses, came upon a sign of their presence that was quite recent. Before following the clew, he communicated his success to his companions; and while the latter were consulting on the circumstance, the youth reappeared, leading the two fillies, with their saddles broken, and the housings soiled, as though they had been permitted to run at will for several days.

"What should this prove?" said Duncan, turning pale, and glancing his eyes around him, as if he feared the brush and leaves were about to give up some horrid secret.

末了的摩希干人

一條山溪或地勢可以用得着這樣的詭計時，他們是要利用的；但是追趕的人很少得受欺，絕不會不看出他們自己的錯誤，誤走不多時，或誤走不遠，就曉得了。

　　到了午後三四點鐘，他們過了斯卡倫斯，向西跟着日落的方向走。他們從一個高處走到底下，那裏有一條急流的溪水流過，他們忽然到了狡狐的徒衆停頓地方，（法蘭西人稱馬伽爲 Le Renand Subtile 卽狡狐——譯者註。）在一個山泉左右有許多滅了的燒過的木片，還有一頭鹿的許多碎肉，肝腸等等，摔在那裏，樹木還有顯明的形迹，是曾被馬匹嚙過的。哈華特在不遠地方找着有樹蔭的地方，他願意相信是柯爾拉（Cora）及阿立斯（Alice 這是孟洛的兩個女兒的名字——譯者註。）休息地方，他在那裏用溫柔的情緒冥想。地上誠然是有人跳過的，四面誠然有顯而可見人與獸的足跡，行踪卻忽然中止了。

　　追蹤這些那拉甘塞（Narragansetts 種族名，又是該種人所住的海灣名，又是一種善於負重的馬名——譯者註。）原是易事，他們好像任意亂走，並無引路的人，不然，只志在求食，並無其他目的。後來安伽斯父子努力找那幾匹馬的行蹤，還是安伽斯找着他們很新近的蹤跡。他先把他所找着的蹤跡告訴他的同伴，才去追蹤；他的同伴們正在討論這個環境的時候，安伽斯又回來，領着兩匹鞍轡已破，馬被已汙的小牝馬，好像是得以任意遊行了好幾天的。

　　旦肯變作臉無人色，四圍看看，好像小樹林及樹葉要揭露可怕的祕密一般，他說道，『這該證明什麼。』

13

THE LAST OF THE MOHICANS

"That our march is come to a quick end, and that we are in an enemy's country," returned the scout. "Had the knave been pressed, and the gentle ones wanted horses to keep up with the party, he might have taken their scalps; but without an enemy at his heels, and with such rugged beasts as these, he would not hurt a hair of their heads. I know your thoughts, and shame be it to our color that you have a reason for them; but he who thinks that even a Mingo would ill-treat a woman unless it be to tomahawk her, knows nothing of Indian natur', or the laws of the woods. No, no; I have heard that the French Indians had come into these hills to hunt the moose, and we are getting within scent of their camp. Why should they not? The morning and evening guns of Ty may be heard any day among these mountains; for the Frenchers are running a new line atween the provinces of the king and the Canadas. It is true that the horses are here, but the Hurons are gone; let us, then, hunt for the path by which they departed."

Hawkeye and the Mohicans now applied themselves to their task in good earnest.[1] A circle of a few hundred feet in circumference was drawn, and each of the party took a segment for his portion. The examination, however, resulted in no discovery. The impressions of footsteps were numerous, but they all appeared like those of men who had wandered about the spot, without any design to quit it. Again the scout and his companions made the circuit of the halting place, each slowly following the other, until they assembled in the centre once more, no wiser than when they started.

---

[1] in good earnest 極 認 眞.

14

末 了 的 摩 希 干 人

探子回答道，『這是證明我們到了一個仇敵的國，我們的進行完得很快。假使我們曾緊緊追趕那個惡棍，那兩個女子無馬，追不上那羣土人，他很許可以取了她們的頭頂皮；但是並無仇人尾追他，他們的馬又是性子烈的，他是不會傷害她們頭上一條頭髮的。我曉得你的思想，你旣有理由發生那種思想，是我們白人應該慚愧的；但凡一個人會想到一個明哥人（Mingo 北美一種土人——譯者註。）會虐待一個女人，除非是用戰斧打死她，就是不曉得土人的性情，不然就是不曉得樹林的法律。（這是勸旦肯不要害怕土人會強奸那兩個女子——譯者註。）不會的，不會的；我曾聽說歸附法蘭西的土人曾到這些山上打大鹿，我們離他們的駐紮地很近了。他們為什麼不該在那裏？在這裏的山上無論那一天都可以聽見泰（地名——譯者註。）地方的早炮及晚炮；因為法蘭西人正在我們君主的幾省及加拿大之間劃一條新線。馬匹誠然在這裏，但是胡倫人已經走了；我們要找尋他們離開此地所走的路。』

鷹眼同這個摩希干人極認眞辦這件事。於是劃一個周圍幾百尺的圓圈，各人察看一部分。結果還是找尋不出。脚迹有許多，好像都在那裏走來走去，並無有離開此地的用意。探子與他的同伴們循環察看停留的地方，一個挨一個慢慢的看，後來又聚在中央，如同初時那樣毫無所得。

15

"Such cunning is not without its deviltry,"[1] exclaimed Hawkeye, when he met the disappointed looks of his assistants.

"We must get down to it, Sagamore, beginning at the spring, and going over the ground by inches. The Huron shall never brag in his tribe that he has a foot which leaves no print."

Setting the example himself,[2] the scout engaged in the scrutiny with renewed zeal. Not a leaf was left unturned.[3] The sticks were removed, and the stones lifted; for Indian cunning was known frequently to adopt these objects as covers, laboring with the utmost patience and industry, to conceal each footstep as they proceeded. Still no discovery was made. At length Uncas, whose activity had enabled him to achieve his portion of the task the soonest, raked the earth across the turbid little rill which ran from the spring, and diverted its course into another channel. So soon as its narrow bed below the dam was dry, he stooped over it with keen and curious eyes. A cry of exultation immediately announced the success of the young warrior. The whole party crowded to the spot where Uncas pointed out the impression of a moccasin in the moist alluvion.

"The lad will be an honor to his people," said Hawkeye, regarding the trail with as much admiration as a naturalist would expend on the tusk of a mammoth or the rib of a mastodon; "ay, and a thorn in the sides of the Hurons. Yet that is not the footstep of an Indian! the weight is too much on the heel, and the toes are squared, as though one

---

[1] deviltry 邪術; 毒計.　[2] Setting the example himself 以身作則.
[3] not a leaf was left unturned 無論什麼都看到了 (這裏可以用字面的意思說塊塊樹葉都翻過來看).

16

末 了 的 摩 希 干 人

　　當鷹眼看見他的幫手們的失望神色，喊道，『這樣的狡詐，並非是無毒計的。』

　　『酋長，我們必得打探到底，在山泉那裏起，逐寸逐寸的細看。我們絕不讓那個胡倫人在他的部落裏頭誇口，說他雖然有脚，卻是不留脚迹的。』

　　探子以身作則，重振熱心，詳細察看。無論什麼都看到了，地上的樹葉，無一片不翻過來看過。樹枝都挪開了；凡是石頭都舉起看過；因爲他們曉得印度人狡詐，常用樹枝及石頭作遮蓋，極其耐煩耐勞的當他們前進時，一步一步的遮蓋他們的脚迹。雖然這樣細心找尋，還是找不出什麼來。後來還是安伽斯的活動，使他最早能夠建立他那一部分的功勞，他把一條從山泉出來的細流的土掘起來，堆在一處塞住了，使其另流入一條水路。一等到在他所造的隈下的水道乾了，他就低頭用尖利的及好察的眼細看。他很得意的喊了一聲，立刻就宣布這個少年戰士的功績。全羣的人都聚在這裏看安伽斯所指出在涇泥上的鹿皮鞋的印像。

　　鷹眼很稱讚這個蹤迹，如同一個自然科學家稱讚荒古時代巨象的牙或蝦蟆龍的一條肋骨；（這種文章當以作者爲獨步──譯者註。）他說道，『這個孩子，將來是他本部族的一個出色人物，又是胡倫人身上的一條刺。可惜這不是一個土人的脚迹！脚跟用力太重，是方頭鞋的脚迹，

of the French dancers had been in, pigeon-winging[1] his tribe! Run back, Uncas, and bring me the size of the singer's foot. You will find a beautiful print of it just opposite yon rock, agin the hillside."

While the youth was engaged in this commission, the scout and Chingachgook were attentively considering the impressions. The measurements agreed, and the former unhesitatingly pronounced that the footstep was that of David, who had once more been made to exchange his shoes for moccasins.

"I can now read the whole of it, as plainly as if I had seen the arts of Le Subtil," he added; "the singer being a man whose gifts lay chiefly in his throat and feet, was made to go first, and the others have trod in his steps, imitating their formation."

"But," cried Duncan, "I see no signs of—"

"The gentle ones," interrupted the scout; "the varlet has found a way to carry them until he supposed he had thrown any followers off the scent. My life on it, we see their pretty little feet again, before many rods go by."

The whole party now proceeded, following the course of the rill, keeping anxious eyes on the regular impressions. The water soon flowed into its bed again, but watching the ground on either side, the foresters pursued their way content with knowing that the trail lay beneath. More than half a mile was passed, before the rill rippled close around the base of an extensive and dry rock. Here they paused to make sure that the Hurons had not quitted the water.

---

[1] pigeon-winging 一種跳舞名.

末　了　的　摩　希　干　人

好像有一個法蘭西跳舞人曾進來，拉住他的部落跳舞！安伽斯，你跑回頭把唱歌人的腳的尺寸給我。山邊的石頭對過有他的很好的足跡。』

當這個少年走去辦這件事的時候，探子與慶伽谷留心考慮那些足跡。尺寸是相符的，探子並不遲疑就宣布是大衛的足跡，有人再叫他換了鹿皮鞋，不穿他的鞋子。

探子說道，『我現在能夠很清楚的解說這件事，如同我親眼看見狡狐使手段一樣；唱歌人的本事全在他的喉嚨與他的兩腳，他們叫他先走，其餘的人在他的足跡上走，學他的腳步。』

旦肯喊道，『但是我看不見足跡……。』

探子打义說道，『那個奴才想出一個法子抬小姐們過去，等到他猜任何尾隨的人已經失了蹤跡，才不抬。我敢說，我們向前再走幾十碼，又會看見她們的小腳。』

現在全隊的人向前走，跟着細流的方向走，很留心看整齊的足跡。那條水不久又流入原來的漕，這些獵人留心兩邊看，往前走，曉得所尋的行蹤在水下。他們走過半哩多路，才看見那條細流繞着一塊大而乾的石頭底下流。他們停在這裏，要曉得胡倫人實在並未離開這條水。

It was fortunate they did so. For the quick and active Uncas soon found the impression of a foot on a bunch of moss, where it would seem an Indian had inadvertently trodden. Pursuing the direction given by this discovery, he entered the neighboring thicket, and struck the trail, as fresh and obvious as it had been before they reached the spring. Another shout announced the good fortune of the youth to his companions, and at once terminated the search.

"Ay, it has been planned with Indian judgment," said the scout, when the party was assembled around the place, "and would have blinded white eyes."

"Shall we proceed?" demanded Heyward.

"Softly, softly: we know our path; but it is good to examine the formation of things. This is my schooling, major; and if one neglects the book, there is little chance of learning from the open hand of Providence. All is plain but one thing, which is the manner that the knave contrived to get the gentle ones along the blind trail. Even a Huron would be too proud to let their feet touch the water."

"Will this assist in explaining the difficulty?" said Heyward, pointing toward the fragments of a sort of hand-barrow, that had been rudely constructed of boughs, and bound together with withes, and which now seemed carelessly cast aside as useless.

" 'Tis explained!" cried the delighted Hawkeye. "If them varlets have passed a minute, they have spent hours in striving to fabricate a lying end to their trail! Well, I've known them to waste a day in the same manner, to as little purpose. Here we have three pair of moccasins, and two of little feet. It is amazing that any mortal beings

末　了　的　摩　希　干　人

　　幸而他們停在這裏。因爲敏捷而活勤的安伽斯不久就在一堆苔上找着一個腳印，好像是一個印度人無意中所跳的。他跟着這樣的揭露所指示的方向走，走入附近一個小樹林，就找着行蹤，與在未到山泉之先的行蹤一樣的新鮮及顯露。他又喊一聲，宣布他的好運，給他的同伴們曉得，於是立刻停止追尋。

　　探子當衆人環繞這個地方的時候，說道，『呀，這是用印度人的盤算計劃的，白人的眼睛是會盲目無睹的。』

　　哈華特問道，『我們還往前走麽？』

　　探子說道，『輕點說，輕點說：我們曉得我們的路徑了，但是我們宜於考察是怎樣擺佈的。大佐，這是我的功課；倘若忽略了這本書，就沒得什麽機會從上天的明白指示，得到什麽學問。現在樣樣都明白了，只有一件事未曾明白，那個奴才是用什麽方法使兩位小姐走過無表示的行蹤。卽使是一個胡倫人，也是很驕傲的，不肯涉水走的。』

　　哈華特指着一種手車的碎塊，說道，『這樣東西能否幫助解說爲難？』這架手車是用樹枝粗粗製成，用軟枝細縶的，現在是無用了，隨便摔在一邊。

　　那個得意的鷹眼說道，『解說了！倘若那些奴才們只要一分鐘工夫走過，他們卻曾費了幾點鐘工夫製造這個東西，作爲他們的行蹤的欺人收場！我卻曉得他們曾這樣糟塌一天工夫造很少用處的事。我們看見這裏有三對鹿皮鞋，兩對是小腳的。無論什麽人，那裏能夠用這樣的小

21

can journey on limbs so small! Pass me the thong of buck-skin, Uncas, and let me take the length of this foot. By the Lord, it is no longer than a child's and yet the maidens are tall and comely. That Providence is partial in its gifts, for its own wise reasons, the best and most contented of us must allow."

"The tender limbs of my daughters are unequal to those hardships," said Munro, looking at the light footsteps of his children, with a parent's love; "we shall find their fainting forms in this desert."

"Of that there is little cause of fear," returned the scout, slowly shaking his head; "this is a firm and straight, though a light step, and not over long. See, the heel had hardly touched the ground; and there the dark-hair has made a little jump, from root to root. No, no; my knowledge for it, neither of them was nigh fainting, hereaway. Now, the singer was beginning to be foot-sore and leg-weary, as is plain by his trail. There, you see, he slipped; here he has travelled wide and tottered; and there again it looks as though he journeyed on snow-shoes. Ay, ay, a man who uses his throat altogether, can hardly give his legs a proper training."

From such undeniable testimony did the practised woodsman arrive at the truth, with nearly as much certainty and precision as if he had been a witness of all those events which his ingenuity so easily elucidated.[1] Cheered by these assurances, and satisfied by a reasoning that was so obvious, while it was so simple, the party resumed its course, after making a short halt, to take a hurried repast.

When the meal was ended, the scout cast a glance

[1] elucidated 解 明.

脚走路，未免太令人驚異了！安伽斯，你把鹿皮帶遞給我，讓我量這隻脚有多少長。這還不如小孩子的脚那樣長，但是兩位小姐身材是高的，是好看的。天之所賦是偏袒的，自有其明顯的理由，最好的及最知足的人，必定要承認。』

　　孟洛，帶着爲父的親愛，看了他的兩個女兒的輕的足跡，說道，『我兩個女兒的嬌嫩脚，不能受這樣的辛苦，我們將在沙漠裏找着她們暈倒在地。』

　　探子搖頭，答道，『你有多少理由害怕她們暈倒，這個脚步雖如是輕的，又是不甚長的，卻是有力的，又是直的。你看，脚跟幾乎並不着地；黑髮人在這裏從樹根到樹根，小跳一步。不會的，不會的，我有數，這樣走法，無論那一位小姐都還不至於在這裏暈倒。唱歌人卻起首走到脚痛，兩脚無力了，看他行蹤，就明白。你看，他在這裏失足跌倒；這裏他太往外走，又走得不穩；他走到那裏，好像是穿雪鞋走的。是呀，一個人只管專用喉嚨，就不能夠操練他的脚。』

　　這個有閱歷的獵人就是從這樣不能否認的憑據，得到眞實情形，他料得準確實在，好像是他曾親眼目睹他的聰明所這樣容易解明的事體。這一羣人被這樣的信以爲實所鼓舞，又滿意於這樣顯明而淺近的道理，只停留一會兒，匆匆吃點東西，又往前走。

　　當吃完的時候，探子抬頭看看落山的太陽，很快的前

upward at the setting sun, and pushed forward with a rapidity which compelled Heyward, and the still vigorous Munro to exert all their muscles to equal.[1]　Their route now lay along the bottom which has already been mentioned.　As the Hurons had made no further efforts to conceal their footsteps, the progress of the pursurers was no longer delayed by uncertainty.　Before an hour had elapsed, however, the speed of Hawkeye sensibly abated, and his head, instead of maintaining its former direct and forward look, began to turn suspiciously from side to side, as if he were conscious of approaching danger.　He soon stopped again, and waited for the whole party to come up.

"I scent the Hurons," he said, speaking to the Mohicans; "yonder is open sky, through the tree-tops, and we are getting too nigh to their encampment.　Sagamore, you will take the hillside, to the right; Uncas will bend along the brook to the left, while I will try the trail.　If anything should happen, the call will be three croaks of a crow.　I saw one of the birds fanning himself in the air, just beyond the dead oak—another sign that we are touching an encampment."

The Indians departed their several ways without reply, while Hawkeye cautiously proceeded with the two gentlemen.　Heyward soon pressed to the side of their guide, eager to catch an early glimpse of those enemies he had pursued with so much toil and anxiety.　His companion told him to steal to the edge of the wood, which, as usual, was fringed with a thicket, and wait his coming, for he wished to examine certain suspicious signs a little on one side.　Duncan obeyed, and soon found himself in a situation

---

[1] to equal 趕 快; 趕 上.

行，這就強逼哈華特及精力還強健的孟洛用盡他們的筋力，趕快趕路。現在他們所走的路是沿前文所說的谷底走。因爲胡倫人不再努力遮掩他們的足跡，追蹤的人們的進步不復被懷疑所阻滯。還未走夠一點鐘，鷹眼的進步已經見得慢了些，他的頭本來是直直的向前望，現在起首有點懷疑，兩邊的看，好像曉得有危險到來。他不久又站着，等全羣人走來。

他對摩希干人們說道，『我料胡倫人就在前面；從樹頂就看見那邊是開豁的天，我們走得太近他們紮營地方。酋長，請你在右手的山邊走；安伽斯轉向，沿左手的小溪走，我一面試跟他們的行蹤走。倘有事發生，以三聲鴉叫爲號。我看見一鴉在空中飛，剛在死橡樹那邊——這又是我們走近一個駐紮地的又一記號。』

印度人不答話就分路走了，鷹眼同着兩個白人小心向前走。哈華特不久就逼近他們的嚮導身邊，急於要瞰見他受盡許多辛苦及着急所追逐的仇人們。他的同伴叫他偷偷走到樹林邊（同通常的樹林一樣，邊上有一個小樹林），叫他在那裏等他來，因爲他想察看在一邊的可疑的形跡。旦肯聽他的吩咐，不久就到了一個所在，能夠看見

to command a view which he found as extraordinary as it was novel.

The trees of many acres had been felled, and the glow of a mild summer's evening had fallen on the clearing, in beautiful contrast to the gray light of the forest. A short distance from the place where Duncan stood, the stream had seemingly expanded into a little lake, covering most of the low land, from mountain to mountain. The water fell out of this wide basin, in a cataract so regular and gentle, that it appeared rather to be the work of human hands than fashioned by nature. A hundred earthen dwellings stood on the margin of the lake, and even in its water, as though the latter had overflowed its usual banks. Their rounded roofs, admirably moulded for defence against the weather, denoted more of industry and fore-sight than the natives were wont to bestow on their regular habitations, much less on those they occupied for the temporary purposes of hunting and war. In short, the whole village or town, whichever it might be termed, possessed more of method and neatness of execution, than the white men had been accustomed to believe belonged, ordinarily, to the Indian habits. It appeared, however, to be deserted. At least, so thought Duncan for many minutes; but, at length, he fancied he discovered several human forms advancing toward him on all fours, and apparently dragging in their train some heavy, and as he was quick to apprehend, some formidable engine. Just then a few dark-looking heads gleamed out of the dwellings, and the place seemed suddenly alive with beings, which, however, glided from cover to cover so swiftly, as to allow no opportunity of examining their humors[1] or pursuits. Alarmed

[1] humors 脾氣; 喜怒.

非常而新鮮的光景。

　　他看見有好幾畝的地方的樹木都砍了，一派溫和夏天傍晚的陽光，照在無樹的空地，與樹林的灰色光反襯；離旦肯所站的地方不遠，那條溪流好像發展爲一個小湖，蓋住從這邊山到那邊山的大部分的低地。水從這個湖流出，成爲一個形狀整齊而水流和緩的瀑布，好像是人工所造成的，而不似天然的。湖邊有一百所泥房子，水裏也有，好像是湖水泛濫出隄一般。房頂是圓的，用以躲避風雨是很可嘉的，土人們對於他們的正式住所，還沒有這樣的用力，還沒有這樣的先見，至於他們因爲打獵及打仗所住的臨時寓所更不必說了。說句簡單話，全座鄉村或市鎮（無論怎樣稱謂）頗有建築的方法，及手工的乾淨，多過於白人所習慣相信印度人的積習所常有的。但是這許多房舍好像無人居住。旦肯有幾分鐘至少也是這樣想；但是後來他以爲他看見有幾個人形，四肢到地向着他前進，好像在他們的背後拉重東西，他的悟性靈敏，以爲拖的是一部可怕的機器。剛好這個時候有幾個黑頭從房舍伸出來，那片地方有許多人，忽然熱鬧起來，他們走得很快，從這個房頂溜到那個房頂，並不給他機會留心觀察他們的喜怒或

27

at these suspicious and inexplicable movements, he was about to attempt the signal of the crows, when the rustling of leaves at hand drew his eyes in another direction.

The young man started, and recoiled a few paces instinctively,[1] when he found himself within a hundred yards of a stranger Indian. Recovering his recollection on the instant, instead of sounding an alarm, which might prove fatal to himself, he remained stationary, an attentive observer of the other's motions.

An instant of calm observation served to assure Duncan that he was undiscovered.[2] The native, like himself, seemed occupied in considering the low dwellings of the village, and the stolen movements of its inhabitants. It was impossible to discover the expression of his features, through the grotesque mask of paint under which they were concealed; though Duncan fancied it was rather melancholy than savage. His head was shaved, as usual, with the exception of the crown, from whose tuft three or four faded feathers from a hawk's wing were loosely dangling. A ragged calico mantle half encircled his body, while his nether garment was composed of an ordinary shirt, the sleeves of which were made to perform the office that is usually executed by a much more commodious arrangement. His legs were bare, and sadly cut and torn by briers. The feet were, however, covered with a pair of good deer-skin moccasins. Altogether, the appearance of the individual was forlorn and miserable.

Duncan was still curiously observing the person of his neighbor, when the scout stole silently and cautiously to his side.

---

[1] instinctively 出于自然的; 不由自主的. [2] undiscovered 不曾被人看見.

操作。他看見這許多可疑的及不能解說的動作，就恐怖起來，正想作三聲烏鴉叫以告警，聽見身邊的樹葉作沙剌沙剌聲響，使他兩眼另看他處。

這個少年驚了一跳，不由自主的跳後幾步，看見一個外路的印度人離他不過一百碼。他立刻恢復他的鎮靜，並不報警，（報警許可以送了他自己的性命）他站着不動，專心觀察那個人的動作。

一會兒的鎮靜觀察就使旦肯相信對面的人並未看見他。那個土人，同他自己一樣，好像也是在那裏察看那個村莊的矮房子，和那裏居民的偷偷摸摸的舉動。對面那個人塗了滿臉顏料，旦肯所以看不清他的面目，但是旦肯以爲那個人只是滿面愁容，卻並不野蠻。他的頭髮是薙了，只餘頭頂未薙，從頭頂鬆鬆的垂下三四根鵰翼的退色的羽。一件破爛布衫半圍着他的身子，內衣不過是一件平常的汗衫，他把兩袖拿來作別的用，更爲寬大利便的衣服是不會這樣借用兩袖的。他精着兩脛，兩脛被荊棘所剌傷，傷得利害。兩脚卻穿上一雙很好的鹿皮鞋。總而言之，這個人的面目是可憐的。

旦肯還是出於好意的，觀察這個近在身邊的人的本身，那時候探子小心的及不響的偷偷走到他身邊。

THE LAST OF THE MOHICANS

"You see we have reached their settlement or encampment," whispered the young man; "and here is one of the savages himself, in a very embarrassing position for our further movements."

Hawkeye started, and dropped his rifle, when, directed, by the finger of his companion, the stranger came under his view. Then lowering the dangerous muzzle he stretched forward his long neck, as if to assist a scrutiny that was already intensely keen.

"The imp is not a Huron," he said, "nor of any of the Canada tribes; and yet you see, by his clothes, the knave has been plundering a white. Ay, Montcalm has raked the woods for his inroad, and a whooping, murdering set of varlets has he gathered together. Can you see where he has put his rifle or his bow?"

"He appears to have no arms; nor does he seem to be viciously inclined. Unless he communicate the alarm to his fellows, who, as you see, are dodging about[1] the water, we have but little to fear from him."

The scout turned to Heyward, and regarded him a moment with unconcealed amazement. Then opening wide his mouth, he indulged in unrestrained and heartfelt laughter, though in that silent and peculiar manner which danger had so long taught him to practice.

Repeating the words, "Fellows who are dodging about the water!" he added, "so much for schooling and passing a boyhood in the settlements! The knave has long legs, though, and shall not be trusted. Do you keep him under your rifle while I creep in behind, through the bush, and take him alive. Fire on no account."[2]

---

[1] dodging about 躲躲閃閃的走.　　[2] on no account 無論怎樣都不可.

末 了 的 摩 希 干 人

這個少年附耳對探子說道,『你曉得我們已經到了他們的僑居地或駐紮地,這裏有一個野人,令我們難以耳進行。』

鷹眼一驚,放下他的鎗, 那時候他的同伴指給他看,那個怪人走來,讓他看見。他於是放低有危險的鎗口,伸長他的長頸子, 好像要幫助他的已經是用很尖利的眼光觀察。

他說道,『那個小鬼不是一個胡倫人, 也不是任何加拿大部族人;你看他的衣服,卻可以曉得那個惡棍搶刼一個白人。呀,蒙特卡木因爲入犯,掃除樹林,聚集一羣叫喊殺人的奴才。你能看見他在什麽地方擺他的鎗或他的弓?』

『他旣無兵器;又不像是懷惡意的。你看他在水邊曲曲折折躱躱閃閃的走得很快, 除非他把警信傳與他的同伴們,不然,我們用不着怕他。』

探子掉過頭來,帶着顯露的詫異看哈華特一會子。於是張開大口,放量及痛快的大笑,但是他經歷危險爲日甚久,學會一種不響的及特別的笑。

他學哈華特說『有許多人在水邊曲曲折折躱躱閃閃的走得很快,』又說道,『虧你在僑居地學習及做小孩子這許久!那個惡棍有的是長腿,我們不能相信他。我一面穿小樹林,從後面爬過去,你一面拿鎗指住他,我要活捉他。無論怎樣,你可不要開鎗。』

31

Heyward had already permitted his companion to bury part of his person in the thicket, when, stretching forth his arm, he arrested him, in order to ask:—

"If I see you in danger, may I not risk a shot?"

Hawkeye regarded him a moment, like one who knew not how to take the question; then nodding his head, he answered, still laughing, though inaudibly:—

"Fire a whole platoon, major."

In the next moment he was concealed by the leaves. Duncan waited several minutes in feverish impatience, before he caught another glimpse of the scout. Then he reappeared, creeping along the earth, from which his dress was hardly distinguishable, directly in the rear of his intended captive. Having reached within a few yards of the latter, he arose to his feet, silently and slowly. At that instant, several loud blows were struck on the water, and Duncan turned his eyes just in time to perceive that a hundred dark forms were plunging, in a body, into the troubled little sheet. Grasping his rifle his looks were again bent on the Indian near him. Instead of taking the alarm, the unconscious savage stretched forward his neck, as if he also watched the movements about the gloomy lake, with a sort of silly curiosity. In the meantime, the uplifted hand of Hawkeye was above him. But, without any apparent reason, it was withdrawn, and its owner indulged in another long, though still silent, fit of merriment. When the peculiar and hearty laughter of Hawkeye was ended, instead of grasping his victim by the throat, he tapped him lightly on the shoulder, and exclaimed aloud:—

"How now, friend! have you a mind to teach the beavers to sing?"

末 了 的 摩 希 干 人

哈華特已經讓他的同伴在小樹林裏藏着一部分身子，卻伸出手阻住他，以便問他：——

『我若看見你陷入危險，我可以冒險開一鎗麼？』

鷹眼看他一會，好像不曉得怎樣對答；隨後他點頭，一面還是不響的笑，答道：——

『大佐，只管放一排鎗。』

再過一會他就躲在樹葉裏。旦肯如同害熱病那樣的不耐煩，等了幾分鐘，繞覺見探子。隨後他又出現，在地上爬，正在向他所想擒獲的俘虜背後爬，他的衣服的顏色與土色差不多，幾乎辨不出來。他到了那裏，同那個人相離不過幾碼地，他不響的，慢慢的，站起來。這個時候，有幾個很響的打擊打在水上，旦肯掉過頭來，剛好來得及看見有百十個黑東西，全跳入那一小片不安靜的水裏。他抓住他的鎗，他兩眼還是看離他不遠的土人。那個無知覺的野人並不驚恐，反伸出他的頸子，好像他也是留心察看那片黑暗的湖，帶着一種傻子的好奇神色。當下鷹眼高舉他的手，正在這個人的頭上。不料他好像毫無理由的把手縮回去，又不響的大笑一陣，笑得很久。等到鷹眼的特別的與痛快的大笑完了的時候，他並不掐住他的犧牲的咽喉，反輕輕的敲他的肩膀，大聲喊道：——

『朋友， 你現在幹什麼！ 難道你有心要教海狸唱歌麼？』

"Even so," was the ready answer. "It would seem that the Being that gave them power to improve his gifts so well, would not deny them voices to proclaim his praise."

CHAPTER XXXII

"But the plagues shall spread, and funeral fires increase
Till the great king, without a ransom paid,
To her own Chrysa send the black-eyed maid."—Pope.

During the time Uncas was making this disposition of his forces, the woods were as still, and with the exception of those who had met in council, apparently as much untenanted, as when they came fresh from the hands of their Almighty Creator. The eye could range,[1] in every direction, through the long and shadowed vistas[2] of the trees; but nowhere was any object to be seen that did not properly belong to the peaceful and slumbering[3] scenery. Here and there a bird was heard fluttering among the branches of the beeches, and occasionally a squirrel dropped a nut, drawing the startled looks of the party for a moment to the place; but the instant the casual interruption ceased, the passing air was heard murmuring above their heads, along that verdant and undulating surface of forest, which spread itself unbroken, unless by stream or lake, over such a vast region of country. Across the tract of wilderness which lay between the Delawares and the village of their enemies, it seemed as if the foot of man had never trodden, so breathing and deep was the silence in which it lay. But Hawkeye, whose duty led him foremost in the adventure,

[1] range 看得通; 看得透. [2] vistas 兩排樹木間的空處. [3] slumbering 酣睡; 這裏解作安靜.

末 了 的 靡 希 干 人

那個人答道,『是呀,上帝既賜他們權力,他們改進這樣的權力,改得這樣好,上帝不會不賜他們聲音,以便頌揚他。』

〔哈華特以爲是躲藏的土人們,原來是海狸,他所看見的湖,原來是一個海狸戲水的池子; 他所看見的瀑布, 原來是勤力而聰明的海狸所築的隄:他所疑心的一個仇人原來就是他所深信的朋友,教唱聖歌的先生伽末特大衛 Gamut David。在作者的幾部小說裏頭,這一篇是很有名的文章——譯者註。〕

第三十二回　安伽斯之死

這個時候安伽斯正在那裏布置他的隊伍, 樹林裏是毫無動靜,好像是無人居住,如同從造物主宰手裏初出來的時候一樣,除了與聞軍事會議的人們不計外,他人看得是毫無動靜。眼睛只管向四面八方看,從樹木間的長而有影的空處看,都能看得通; 無論看見什麽地方的東西,無有不是屬於太平景象及安靜情形的。耳朵裏聽見一鳥在樹枝間飛來飛去,有時聽見一隻松鼠丟下一枚栗子,驚動這一羣人舉目往那裏看 (這一節描寫耳聞目見的太平無事景象——譯者註。);只要這樣的偶然的打叉一停止,就聽見吹過的風在他們頭上作聲,沿着樹林的青綠的及如同波浪起伏的面上吹去,這樣的樹林是接連一望無際的,除非是被一條溪流及一個湖所間斷。在狄拉維爾 Dela-wares 人及他們的仇敵的村落之間的一片曠野, 好像是向無人跡的,是一片很沉寂的地方。但是鷹眼在這次的出發要走在衆人的最前頭,卻曉得他所與對敵的人們的性

THE LAST OF THE MOHICANS

knew the character of those with whom he was about to contend too well to trust the treacherous quiet.

When he saw his little band collected, the scout threw "Killdeer"[1] into the hollow of his arm, and making a silent signal that he would be followed, he led them many rods toward the rear, into the bed of a little brook they had crossed in advancing. Here he halted, and after waiting for the whole of his grave and attentive warriors to close about him, he spoke in Delaware, demanding:—

"Do any of my young men know whither this run will lead us?"

A Delaware stretched forth a hand, with the two fingers separated, and indicating the manner in which they were joined at the root, he answered:—

"Before the sun could go his own length, the little water will be in the big." Then he added, pointing in the direction of the place he mentioned, "the two make enough for the beavers,"

"I thought as much," returned the scout, glancing his eye upward at the opening in the tree-tops, "from the course it takes, and the bearings of the mountains. Men, we will keep within the cover of its banks till we scent the Hurons."

His companions gave the usual brief exclamation of assent, but perceiving that their leader was about to lead the way in person, one or two made signs that all was not as it should be. Hawkeye, who comprehended their meaning glances, turned and perceived that his party had been followed thus far by the singing-master.

---

[1] Killdeer 鎗名.

格,不相信這樣欺人的寂靜。

　　當這個探子看見他的一小隊的人齊集時候,就夾住他的長鎗,發一個暗號,要衆人跟隨他,他領他們往後走幾十碼,走入他們前進的所穿過的小溪裏。他就在這裏暫停,等候全數他的嚴肅及留心的戰士們靠近他的時候,他就用狄拉維爾話問他們,說道:——

　　『那一個少年曉得這條小溪流向那裏?』

　　有一個狄拉維爾人伸出一隻手,分開兩隻手指,表示兩條小溪在源頭滙合,他答道:——

　　『等到太陽走完了的時候,小溪就流入大河。』他隨卽用手指向他所說的地方又說道,『兩條水足夠海狸居住。』

　　探子舉目看樹頂的開豁地方,答道,『我原想是這樣,看溪流的方向和山的方向,我曉得是這樣。兄弟們,我們用溪流的兩岸作遮護,等到我們曉得胡倫人的所在再說。』

　　他的同伴們同向來一樣,只響了一聲,表示同意,但是他們一看見他們的領袖快要自己領導,有一兩個人做手勢,表示這是不對的。鷹眼理會他們的眼色,就掉過頭來,看見那個唱歌先生跟隨這羣人,跟到這裏。

"Do you know, friend," asked the scout, gravely, and perhaps with a little of the pride of conscious deserving in his manner, "that this is a band of rangers chosen for the most desperate service, and put under the command of one who, though another might say it with a better face, will not be apt to leave them idle? It may not be five, it cannot be thirty minutes before we tread on the body of a Huron, living or dead."

"Though not admonished of your intentions in words," returned David, whose face was a little flushed, and whose ordinarily quiet and unmeaning eyes glimmered with an expression of unusual fire, "your men have reminded me of the children of Jacob going out to battle against the Shechemites, for wickedly aspiring to wedlock with a woman of a race that was favored of the Lord. Now, I have journeyed far, and sojourned much in good and evil with the maiden ye seek; and though not a man of war, with my loins girded and my sword sharpened, yet would I gladly strike a blow in her behalf."

The scout hesitated, as if weighing the chances of such a strange enlistment in his mind before he answered:—

"You know not the use of any we'pon. You carry no rifle; and believe me, what the Mingoes take they will freely give again."

"Though not a vaunting and bloodily disposed Goliath," returned David, drawing a sling from beneath his particolored and uncouth attire, "I have not forgotten the example of the Jewish boy. With this ancient instrument of war have I practised much in my youth, and peradventure the skill has not entirely departed from me."

"Ay!" said Hawyeke, considering the deer-skin thong and apron, with a cold and discouraging eye; "the thing

38

末了的摩希干人

探子鄭重的，還許帶着一點自以爲是的態度，問道，『朋友，你曉得麼我們是一個遊擊隊，精選做最危險的事，歸一個人統帶，別人雖然可以有更好的資格說，這個人卻是不會使他們無事做的？也許不過五分鐘，絕不能過半點鐘，我們就可以跐着一個活的或死的胡倫的身體。』

大衛聽了，臉上有點發紅，他的眼色向來是安靜的，無意義的，到了這個時候，冒出非常的火氣，答道，『你所統領的人們使我追憶雅各的苗裔出去同示劍人打仗，因爲其中有一個人心懷不良，要同上帝所優待的種族的一個女子結婚。（事見舊約創世記——譯者註。）我是走過很遠地方的人，我曾同你所尋找的女子無論在太平及不太平的時候相處日久；我雖然不是一個打仗的人，我只要束住我的腰，磨利我的刀子，我是很高興替她出力，打一仗。』

探子遲疑一會，好像要在心裏盤算過這樣的一個怪人入伍的得失，才肯答他。

探子於是說道，『你不曉得用什麽兵器。你手上無鎗，我對你實說，明哥人受人打，是會很自由還手的。』

大衛從他的雜色衣服及難看的裝束裏頭，掏出一條擲石繩子來，答道，『我雖然不如坷利亞（Goliath）那樣誇口，又不如他那樣好流血，（事見舊約——譯者註。）我卻不曾忘記那個猶太孩子的榜樣。我少年時曾很練習這樣古時的兵器，很許我還未整個的忘記了我的本事。』

鷹眼看看大衛的鹿皮腰帶和鹿皮的帷裙，帶着冷淡及不滿意的眼色，說道，『唉！敵人用箭或用刀，這件東西

might do its work among arrows, or even knives: but these Mengwe have been furnished by the Frenchers with a grooved barrel a man. However, it seems to be your gift to go unharmed amid fire, and as you have hitherto been favored—major, you have left your rifle at a cock; a single shot before the time would be just twenty scalps lost to no purpose—singer, you can follow; we may find use for you in the shoutings."

"I thank you, friend," returned David, supplying himself, like royal namesake, from among the pebbles of the brook; "though not given to the desire to kill, had you sent me away my spirit would have been troubled."

"Remember," added the scout, tapping his own head significantly on that spot where Gamut was yet sore, "we come to fight, and not to musickate. Until the general whoop is given, nothing speaks but the rifle."

David nodded, as much as to signify his acquiescence with the terms; and then Hawkeye, casting another observant glance over his followers, made the signal to proceed.

Their route lay, for the distance of a mile, along the bed of the water-course. Though protected from any great danger of observation by the precipitous banks, and the thick shrubbery which skirted the stream, no precaution known to an Indian attack was neglected. A warrior rather crawled than walked on each flank, so as to catch occasional glimpses into the forest; and every few minutes the band came to a halt, and listened for hostile sounds, with an acuteness of organs that would be scarcely conceivable to a man in a less natural state. Their march was, however, unmolested, and they reached the point where the lesser stream was lost in the greater, without

還許可以有點用處：但是孟貴人（卽明哥人——譯者註。）得了法蘭西人的接濟，每人都有一桿鎗。雖是這樣說，你好像是得着一種天賜，在鎗林彈雨裏頭是不會受傷的，你一向得過這種便宜，——少佐，你的鎗是扳了機預備放；未到時先放鎗就是白糟塲子彈，就是失了二十塊頭頂皮——唱歌先生，你可以跟我們走，當大喊的時候你許可以有點用處。』

　　大衛學新約的大衞王，果然在溪裏拾許多石子，說道『朋友，我謝了你；我雖然不想殺人，但是假使你把我鬧走了，我心裏是很不安的。』

　　探子敲敲自己的頭，特爲敲伽末特覺得還痛的那一塊，說道，『你要記得，我們是去打仗，不是去奏音樂。要等到同時吶喊的時候，你才好唱歌，未到這個時候，只許鎗說話。』

　　大衛點頭，好像表示他肯履行這樣的條件；鷹眼留意看他的部下，就發號前進。（這幾段作者嘗試作有諧趣的文章——譯者註。）

　　他們所走的路有一哩遠是沿溪底前進。雖然有溪流的兩邊陡岸及圍繞這條溪的深密灌木所遮護，不會有被敵人看見的大險，他們曉得印度人攻打的方法，在在都要預防，毫不忽略。一個打仗的人其實是在兩旁爬，並不是走，以便隨時窺見樹林；每幾分鐘就停頓一會，以便留心聽敵人的動靜，他們的聽官很尖利，不是在這樣野地的人，是不會想到會這樣尖利的。他們前進，不曾遇着什麼騷擾，走到小溪流入大河的地點，並無憑證表示有人曉得

the smallest evidence that their progress had been noted. Here the scout again halted, to consult the signs of the forest.

"We are likely to have a good day for a fight," he said, in English, addressing Heyward, and glancing his eyes upward at the clouds, which began to move in broad sheets across the firmament; "a bright sun and a glittering barrel are no friends to true sight. Everything is favorable; they have the wind, which will bring down their noises and their smoke, too, no little matter in itself; whereas, with us it will be first a shot, and then a clear view. But here is an end to our cover; the beavers have had the range of this stream for hundreds of years, and what atween their food and their dams, there is, as you see, many a girdled stub, but few living trees."

Hawkeye had, in truth, in these few words, given no bad description of the prospect that now lay in their front. The brook was irregular in its width, sometimes shooting through narrow fissures in the rocks, and at others spreading over acres of bottom land, forming little areas that might be termed ponds. Everywhere along its banks were the mouldering relics of dead trees, in all the stages of decay, from those that groaned on their tottering trunks to such as had recently been robbed of those rugged coats that so mysteriously contain their principle of life. A few long, low, and moss-covered piles were scattered among them, like the memorials of a former and long-departed generation.

All these minute particulars were noted by the scout, with a gravity and interest that they probably had never before attracted. He knew that the Huron encampment lay a short half mile up the brook; and with the characteristic

他們的進行。探子到了這裏又暫停，討論樹林的表示。

　　他舉目看天上的雲，那時候許多雲成爲好幾大片在天上走過，他用英語對哈華特說道，『我們很許有一好天打仗，一片光亮的太陽，及一支發亮的鎗，是不容易描準的。事事都是利便的；他們在上風，他們的聲音及濃烟都吹到我們這邊來，這是頗要緊的；至於我們這方面，先放一槍，隨後纔看得清楚。我們這時候到了無遮護的地方了；海狸們據有這條溪流有好幾百年了，他們旣要吃又要築堤，什麼東西都給他們用光了，只有幾捆的殘餘樹根，很少活的樹了。』

　　鷹眼所說的不過是少少的幾句話，其實把眼前的光景寫得並不壞。溪流是寬窄不等的，有時從窄的石縫穿過，有時放大了鋪在好幾畝的地上，成爲許多小片，可以稱爲池子。兩岸隨處都是發黴的死樹的殘餘，有起首朽腐的，有朽腐了多時的，有樹身動搖，快要倒的，有許多樹的擁腫不定的樹皮新近才被海狸銜走，樹皮是很神祕的蘊藏着樹的生命的元素。其間有幾條長而在低處的鋪滿綠苔的木橛，縱橫放着，好像是許久以前的時代的紀念品。

　　探子全注意到這許多詳細情景，他很鄭重的注意，很許向來無人理會到。他曉得胡倫部落的大營在山溪的上游，離此不過半哩路；他怕有埋伏的危險，他特別的煩心，

anxiety[1] of one who dreaded a hidden danger, he was greatly troubled at not finding the smallest trace of the presence of his enemy. Once or twice he felt induced to give the order for a rush, and to attempt the village by surprise; but his experience quickly admonished him of the danger of so useless an experiment. Then he listened intently, and with painful uncertainty, for the sounds of hostility in the quarter where Uncas was left; but nothing was audible except the sighing of the wind, that began to sweep over the bosom of the forest in gusts which threatened a tempest. At length, yielding rather to his unusual impatience than taking counsel from his knowledge, he determined to bring matters to an issue,[2] by unmasking his force, and proceeding cautiously, but steadily, up the stream.

The scout had stood, while making his observations, sheltered by a brake, and his companions still lay in the bed of the ravine, through which the smaller stream debouched; but on hearing his low, though intelligible signal the whole party stole up the bank, like so many dark spectres, and silently arranged themselves around him. Pointing in the direction he wished to proceed, Hawkeye advanced, the band breaking off in single files, and following so accurately in his footsteps, as to leave it, if we except Heyward and David, the trail of but a single man.

The party was, however, scarcely uncovered before a volley from a dozen rifles was heard in their rear; and a Delaware leaping high into the air, like a wounded deer, fell at his whole length, perfectly dead.

"Ah, I feared some deviltry like this!" exclaimed the scout, in English; adding with the quickness of thought, in his adopted tongue: "To cover, men, and charge!"

---

[1] anxiety 煩心.　[2] bring matters to an issue 決勝負.

末 了 的 摩 希 干 人

他看不見一點敵人的蹤跡,心裏很愁悶。有一兩次他想下令衝擊,嘗試襲攻敵人的村落;但是他的閱歷很快的警告他,這樣的無用嘗試很有危險。他於是用心細聽,聽安伽斯所在的那一方面的打仗聲音,心裏搖搖無定,是很難過的;但是聽不見什麼聲音,只聽見風聲,這時候一陣一陣的風起首在樹林中吹過,好像是要刮大風。後來他讓步於他的非常的不耐煩,並不商諸他的知識,就決計不遮掩他的隊伍,小心按步,逆流前進,決個勝負。

當探子觀察情形的時候,他原是站着,有一堆草遮住他,他的同袍們躲在溪底,這是小溪的出口;但是他們一聽見他的聲音雖低而可以聽得清楚的號令,全隊偷偷登岸,好像多少黑暗的鬼影,不聲不響的布置在他的前後左右,鷹眼用手指着他所想前進的方向一面上前,這一羣人就散開,魚貫前進,很準確的跟他腳步走,那一條的腳跡好像是一個人走的,只有哈華特和大衛兩人,不跟着這條行蹤走。

這一羣人幾乎還未盡露面的時候,就聽見後面有一排十二枝鎗的鎗聲;有一個狄拉維爾人跳上空中,跳得很高,好像一條受了傷的鹿,直挺挺倒在地下,死了。

探子說英國話喊道,『哈,我原怕有如這樣的詭計;』他用如同思想那樣的迅速,用土話說道,『你們躲藏起來,放鎗!』

THE LAST OF THE MOHICANS

The band dispersed at the word, and before Heyward had well recovered from his surprise he found himself standing alone with David. Luckily the Hurons had already fallen back, and he was safe from their fire. But this state of things was evidently to be of short continuance; for the scout set the example of pressing on their retreat, by discharging his rifle, and darting from tree to tree as his enemy slowly yielded ground.

It would seem that the assault had been made by a very small party of the Hurons, which, however, continued to increase in numbers, as it retired on its friends, until the return fire was very nearly, if not quite, equal to that maintained by the advancing Delawares. Heyward threw himself among the combatants, and imitating the necessary caution of his companions, he made quick discharges with his own rifle. The contest now grew warm and stationary. Few were injured, as both parties kept their bodies as much protected as possible by the trees; never, indeed, exposing any part of their persons except in the act of taking aim. But the chances were gradually growing unfavorable to Hawkeye and his band. The quick-sighted scout perceived his danger without knowing how to remedy it. He saw it was more dangerous to retreat than to maintain his ground; while he found his enemy throwing out men on his flank, which, rendered the task of keeping themselves covered so very difficult to the Delawares as nearly to silence their fire. At this embarrassing moment, when they began to think the whole of the hostile tribe was gradually encircling them, they heard the yell of combatants and the rattling of arms, echoing under the arches of the wood, at the place where Uncas was posted; a bottom which, in a manner, lay beneath the ground on which Hawkeye and his party were contending.

46

末　了　的　摩　希　干　人

　　這羣人一聽這個號令，就散開，哈華特還驚愕未定，就看見只有他同大衛兩個人獨站在一起。好在胡倫人已經往後退，他們的鎗打不中他。但是這樣的情形顯然是不長久的；因爲探子當他的仇敵慢慢讓步的時候，從這株樹跳到那株樹，做個追趕退後的敵人的榜樣。

　　看來不過是很小數的胡倫人來攻，但是當他們退到他們的朋友們所在的地方，人數卻接連加多，等到後來，他們回敬所放的鎗，幾乎同進攻的狄拉維爾人所放的鎗那樣多。哈華特混在裏頭打仗，學他的同伴們的必須的謹愼，放自己的鎗，放得很快。現在奮鬪得很熱烈，無進無退。受傷的不多，因爲兩方都是盡其所能，用樹木護身；除了瞄準之外，是不露肢體的。但是機會是逐漸不利於鷹眼和他的隊伍。眼快的探子曉得他的危險，卻不曉得怎樣補救。他看出退兵比堅守陣地還要危險得多；同時他看見他的敵人派人出來旁抄，狄拉維爾人就難以護身，幾乎不放鎗了。正在爲難的時候，他們起首以爲全體仇敵的部落正在逐漸包圍他們，他們聽見在樹林交加所成的拱弧之下有戰士們的喊聲及鎗聲，這是在安伽斯所駐在的地方；這是一塊低地，在鷹眼與他的隊伍作戰地方之下。

The effects of this attack were instantaneous, and to the scout and his friends greatly relieving. It would seem that, while his own surprise had been anticipated, and had consequently failed, the enemy, in their turn, having been deceived in its object and in his numbers, had left too small a force to resist the impetuous onset of the young Mohican. This fact was doubly apparent, by the rapid manner in which the battle in the forest rolled upward toward the village, and by an instant falling off in the number of their assailants, who rushed to assist in maintaining the front, and, as it now proved to be, the principal point of defence.

Animating his followers by his voice, and his own example, Hawkeye then gave the word to bear down upon their foes. The charge, in that rude species of warfare, consisted merely in pushing from cover to cover, nigher to the enemy; and in this manœuvre he was instantly and successfully obeyed. The Hurons were compelled to withdraw, and the scene of the contest rapidly changed from the more open ground on which it had commenced to a spot where the assailed found a thicket to rest upon. Here the struggle was protracted, arduous, and seemingly of doubtful issue; the Delawares, though none of them fell, beginning to bleed freely, in consequence of the disadvantage at which they were held.

In this crisis, Hawkeye found means to get behind the same tree as that which served for a cover to Heyward; most of his own combatants being within call, a little on his right, where they maintained rapid, though fruitless, discharges on their sheltered enemies.

"You are a young man, major," said the scout, dropping the butt of "Killdeer" to earth, and leaning on the barrel,

48

末 了 的 摩 希 干 人

這樣的攻打是立刻見效的，探子和他的朋友們得着重要的解救。他的襲擊，原被敵人所預料，所以失敗，但是敵人方面卻誤會他的目的，不曉得他的人數，只留太小的隊伍抗拒這個少年摩希干的奮勇撲攻。這樣的撲攻有兩件事可以證明，一是樹林裏的奮鬪很快的向上滾，滾向村子，二是敵人的人數立刻減少了，他們衝上去幫助維持前線，現在證明這裏是守衛的要點。

鷹眼用他的聲音及榜樣鼓勵他的徒衆，下令擊退他們的仇敵。那樣的粗淺作戰，衝鋒不過是從這個遮護地方衝到那個遮護地方，越衝越近敵人；他的隊伍立刻聽令，果然成功。胡倫人被逼退後，相爭的地點變得很快，初時所爭的是更爲豁露地方，現在所爭的是被攻擊的仇敵們所據的一個叢林。兩方在這裏爭持得長久，爭持得費力，好像是勝負不分；狄拉維爾人雖然並未死一個，卻因他們所據的地點不便利，起首流許多血。

鷹眼到了這個危險當口，設法走到哈華特所利用作遮護的樹後；大多數他自己的打手們都相離不遠，稍微在他的右邊，聲息相通，他們在這裏放鎗攻打他們有遮護的敵人，放得雖快，卻無效果。

探子把他的『殺鹿』鎗杷放在地上，靠着鎗膛，因爲他辛苦了，覺得有點勞倦，說道，『少佐，你是個少年，將來有

a little fatigued with his previous industry; "and it may be your gift to lead armies, at some future day, ag'in these imps, the Mingoes. You may here see the philosophy[1] of an Indian fight. It consists mainly, in a ready hand, a quick eye, and a good cover. Now, if you had a company of the Royal Americans here, in what manner would you set them to work in this business?"

"The bayonet would make a road."

"Ay, there is white reason[2] in what you say; but a man must ask himself, in this wilderness, how many lives he can spare. No—horse," continued the scout, shaking his head, like one who mused; "horse, I am ashamed to say, must sooner or later, decide these scrimmages. The brutes are better than men, and to horse we must come at last. Put a shodden hoof on the moccasin of a red-skin, and if his rifle be once emptied, he will never stop to load it again."

"This is a subject that might better be discussed at another time," returned Heyward; "shall we charge?"

"I see no contradiction to the gifts of any man, in passing his breathing spells in useful reflections," the scout replied. "As to a rush, I little relish such a measure; for a scalp or two must be thrown away in the attempt. And yet," he added, bending his head aside, to catch the sounds of the distant combat, "if we are to be of use to Uncas, these knaves in our front must be got rid of!"

Then turning with a prompt and decided air, he called aloud to his Indians in their own language. His words were answered by a shout; and, at a given signal, each warrior made a swift movement around his particular

---

[1] philosophy 這裏作戰術解.　[2] white reason 好理由.

末　了　的　摩　希　干　人

一天,你也許奉命攻打這些小鬼們,攻打這些明哥人。你在這裏就可以看見同印度人打仗的戰術。最要緊的是眼明手快,及一個好的遮護地方。假使你有一支英國的美洲隊,你同土人打仗該怎樣部署他們?』(作者善於在百忙中故作好整以暇的態度——譯者註。)

『用刺刀殺開一條路。』

『是呀,你說的話未嘗無好理由; 但是一個人在這樣的野地,必要自問他能夠犧牲多少人。』探子搖搖頭,好像是在那裏尋思,接着說道,『不對的,還是不如用馬(作者原注:美洲樹林,無礙馬的小樹林,宜於用馬), 用馬遲早必能決定這樣亂打的勝負,我說這句話覺得難爲情。馬比人強,到了我們必得用馬。用鐵蹄對付土人的鹿皮鞋,倘若他放了一鎗,他絕不肯停留再裝子彈。』

哈華特答道,『我們莫如後來再討論這個問題,我們衝過去嗎?』

探子答道,『一個人借有用的反省作休息,原是無礙於他的天才的。我卻不甚以衝擊爲然;因爲這樣的嘗試必要損失一兩塊頭頂皮。』他卻歪着頭聽遠處打仗的聲音,又說道,『雖是這樣說,我們若要幫助安伽斯,卻不能不打退面前的惡棍們。』

他於是帶着一種麻利和決斷的神氣,掉過頭來,大聲用土話對他的土人說。他們大喊一聲作答:探子給他們一個暗號,每個土人很快的繞過他們各人的樹。同時有這許

tree. The sight of so many dark bodies, glancing before their eyes at the same instant, drew a hasty and consequently an ineffectual fire from the Hurons. Without stopping to breathe, the Delawares leaped in long bounds toward the wood, like so many panthers springing upon their prey. Hawkeye was in front, brandishing his terrible rifle, and animating his followers by his example. A few of the older and more cunning Hurons, who had not been deceived by the artifice which had been practised to draw their fire, now made a close and deadly discharge of their pieces and justified the apprehensions of the scout by felling three of his foremost warriors. But the shock was insufficient to repel the impetus of the charge. The Delawares broke into the cover with the ferocity of their natures and swept away every trace of resistance by the fury of the onset.

The combat endured only for an instant, hand to hand, and then the assailed yielded ground rapidly, until they reached the opposite margin of the thicket, where they clung to the cover, with the sort of obstinacy that is so often witnessed in hunted brutes. At this critical moment, when the success of the struggle was again becoming doubtful, the crack of a rifle was heard behind the Hurons, and a bullet came whizzing from among some beaver lodges, which were situated in the clearing in their rear, and was followed by the fierce and appalling yell of the warwhoop.

"There speaks the Sagamore!" shouted Hawkeye, answering the cry with his own stentorian voice; "we have them now in face and back!"

The effect on the Hurons was instantaneous. Discouraged by an assault from a quarter that left them no

多黑色身子在胡倫人眼前走過,胡倫人就匆匆放鎗,因爲匆匆所以無效果。狄拉維爾人並不停頓以便呼吸,開長脚步向樹林跳,好像許多豹向所欲擒的野獸身上跳。鷹眼在前,舞他的可怕的鎗,以身作則,鼓勵他的徒衆。有幾個年紀較老,又較爲詭詐的胡倫人,並不曾被對方引他們放鎗的詭計所欺,這時候放稠密而命中的鎗,擊死在最前列的三個戰士,果然應了探子的憂慮。但是這樣的打擊,不足以打退衝鋒的兇猛來勢。狄拉維爾人很兇猛的攻入敵人的遮護,他們的瘋狂進攻,掃盡了無論什麼抗拒的蹤跡。

兩方手對手的奮鬪不過一會子就完了,隨後被攻的人們讓步得快,等到他們退到叢林對面的那邊,就死守這個遮護,被獵的野獸,往往表現這樣的死守。正在這個危急的當口,奮鬪的勝負又變作未決的時候,聽見胡倫人的背後有鎗聲,一個鎗子從海狸的窩飛來(這些窩在他們背後的無樹木地方),跟着就是洶洶的及可怕的一陣吶喊。(這幾段是作者的最好文章——譯者註。)

鷹眼用他自己的洪亮聲音,大聲作響應,喊道,『這是酋長放鎗,我們現在是前後夾攻仇敵啦!』

前後夾攻所及於胡倫人的效果,立刻發現。他們的後路被人攻擊,使他們無機會可得遮護,就灰了心, 衆人同

opportunity for cover, the warriors uttered a common yell of disappointment, and breaking off in a body, they spread themselves across the opening, heedless of every considera. tion but flight. Many fell. in making the experiment. under the bullets and the blows of the pursuing Dela. wares.

We shall not pause to detail the meeting between the scout and Chingachgook, or the more touching interview that Duncan held with Munro. A few brief and hurried words served to explain the state of things to both parties; and then Hawkeye pointing out the Sagamore to his band, resigned the chief authority into the hands of the Mohican chief. Chingachgook assumed the station to which his birth and experience gave him so distinguished a claim, with grave dignity that always gives force to the mandates of a native warrior, Following the footsteps of the scout, he led the party back through the thicket, his men scalping the fallen Hurons and secreting the bodies of their own dead as they proceeded, until they gained a point where the former was content to make a halt.

The warriors who had breathed themselves freely in the preceding struggle, were now posted on a bit of level ground, sprinkled with trees in sufficient numbers to con. ceal them. The land fell away rather precipitately in front, and beneath their eyes stretched, for several miles, a narrow, dark, and wooded vale. It was through this dense and dark forest that Uncas was still contending with the main body of the Hurons.

The Mohican and his friends advanced to the brow of the hill, and listened, with practised ears, to the sounds of the combat. A few birds hovered over the leafy bosom of the valley, frightened from their secluded nests; and

喊一聲表現失望，全體逃走，什麼都不顧，只顧逃走，布滿樹林的出路。狄拉維爾人追趕，敵人當嘗試逃走的時候，有中鎗子的，有被擊的，死了好幾個。

探子與慶伽谷相見的詳情，或旦肯與孟洛的更能動人的相會，我們不詳敍了。只要匆匆的說不多幾句的話就能對彼此解說情形；鷹眼隨卽對他的一羣人指着酋長，把兵權交還這個摩希干酋長。慶伽谷就當了統領，他的出身及他的閱歷，給他以這樣高貴的權力，他就任的時候，帶着嚴肅態度，使一個土人的酋長的命令加倍有力。他跟着探子，領着這羣人回頭穿過叢林，他手下的人們一路走一路割取陣亡胡倫人的頭頂皮，掩埋他們自己的陣亡人的屍身，後來走到一個地點，探子願意在這裏停頓。

剛才臨陣未死的戰士們，現時布置在一塊平地上，這裏也有樹，那裏也有樹，足以遮護他們。前面的地很陡的往下斜，在他們的眼底下展長一個窄而黑的有樹木的山谷，有幾哩長。安伽斯還在這裏的深黑的樹林裏頭同胡倫人的大隊奮鬪。

這個摩希干同他的朋友人們前進至山頭，用聽慣的兩耳留心聽打仗的聲音。有不多的幾隻鳥，從深藏的鳥巢裏受了驚，在山谷的樹林上徘徊；從樹上出來的，這裏及

here and there a light vapory cloud, which seemed already blending with the atmosphere, arose above the trees, and indicated some spot where the struggle had been fierce and stationary.

"The fight is coming up the ascent," said Duncan, pointing in the direction of a new explosion of firearms; "we are too much in the center of their line to be effective."

"They will incline into the hollow, where the cover is thicker," said the scout, "and that will leave us well on their flank. Go, Sagamore; you will hardly be in time to give the whoop, and lead on the young men. I will fight this scrimmage with warriors of my own color. You know me, Mohican; not a Huron of them all shall cross the swell, into your rear, without the notice of 'Killdeer.'"

The Indian chief paused another moment to consider the sign of the contest, which was now rolling rapidly up the ascent, a certain evidence that the Delawares triumphed; nor did he actually quit the place until admonished of the proximity of his friends, as well as enemies, by the bullets of the former, which began to patter among the dried leaves on the ground, like the bits of falling hail which precede the bursting of the tempest. Hawkeye and his three companions withdrew a few paces to a shelter, and awaited the issue with calmness that nothing but great practice could impart in such a scene.

It was not long before the reports of the rifles began to lose the echoes of the woods, and to sound like weapons discharged in the open air. Then a warrior appeared, here and there, driven to the skirts of the forest, and rallying as he entered the clearing, as at the place where the final stand was to be made. These were soon joined by others, until a long line of swarthy figures was to be

末 了 的 摩 希 干 人

那裏有薄薄的雲氣,好像已經同空氣混合,這就表示在某地點有人酣戰,還未分勝負。

旦肯指着有鎗子新炸烈的聲音的方向,說道,『他們打上來啦,我們太過在他們戰線的中央,不能得力。』

探子說道,『他們將下去,入山谷,那裏的遮護更密,這就使我們正在他們的側面。酋長,請你去;恐怕你來不及呐喊,領那些少年前進。我用我自己的白人們廝殺。摩希干,你是曉得我的;若有胡倫人過山頭,要走到你的背後,逃不了『殺鹿』的彈子。』

這個印度酋長稍停一會子,考慮奮鬪的現象,這時候這場仗很快的向上滾,這是狄拉維爾人得勝的準確憑據;他等到他的朋友們的鎗子起首落在地下的乾樹葉上,如同狂風初起時先落下的雹子一樣,曉得他的朋友們及仇敵們都走得近了,他才肯實行離開這個地方。鷹眼與他的三個同袍退後幾步,藏在有遮護的地方,很鎮靜的等候結果,看見這樣的光景,非習慣久了的,不能有這樣的鎮靜。

鎗聲不久就無樹林的回響,好像是在空地上放鎗的聲音。隨後就有一個戰士或在這裏或在那裏出現,被逐到樹林邊,當他走入無樹的空地,就在那裏聚合,因為要在那裏作最後的拒守。不久又有許多人來聚,等到後來有一

seen clinging to the cover with the obstinacy of desperation. Heyward began to grow impatient, and turned his eyes anxiously in the direction of Chingachgook. The chief was seated on a rock, with nothing visible but his calm visage, considering the spectacle with an eye as deliberate as if he were posted there merely to view the struggle.

"The time is come for the Delawares to strike!" said Duncan.

"Not so, not so," returned the scout; "when he scents his friends, he will let them know that he is here. See, see; the knaves are getting in that clump of pines, like bees settling after their flight. By the Lord, a squaw might put a bullet into the center of such a knot of dark skins!"

At that instant the whoop was given, and a dozen Hurons fell by a discharge from Chingachgook and his band. The shout that followed was answered by a single war-cry from the forest, and a yell passed through the air that sounded as if a thousand throats were united in a common effort. The Hurons staggered, deserting the center of their line, and Uncas issued from the forest through the opening they left, at the head of a hundred warriors.

Waving his hands right and left, the young chief pointed out the enemy to his followers, who separated in pursuit. The war now divided, both wings of the broken Hurons seeking protection in the woods again, hotly pressed by the victorious warriors of the Lenape. A minute might have passed, but the sounds were already receding in different directions, and gradually losing their distinctness beneath the echoing arches of the woods. One little knot of Hurons, however, had disdained to seek a cover, and were retiring, like lions at bay, slowly and sullenly up the acclivity which

長組的黑人拚命的死守這個遮護地方。哈華特起首不耐煩,掉過臉來,兩眼很着急的往慶伽谷所在的方向看。這個酋長坐在一塊石上, 看不見什麼, 只看見他的鎮靜面目,看眼前的景象,看得很用心, 好像他不過是在那裏看打仗的。

旦肯說道,『 時候到了, 這個狄拉維爾人應該攻打啦。』

探子回道,『不到時候,不到時候,當他看見他的朋友們的時候,他要他們曉得他在這裏。你看呀,你看呀,那這惡棍正在走入那堆杉樹裏, 如同許多密蜂飛走之後停頓下來。天呀, 一個女人就可以向這樣一羣黑人裏頭放一鎗!』

正在這個時候,一聲吶喊,就有十二個胡倫人被慶伽谷和他的部下一排鎗所打倒。隨着鎗聲的大喊,被從樹林出來的一次吶喊所響應,又有一陣喊聲經過空中,好像是一千人合力同時叫喊的。胡倫人逃走,走得快要倒,拋棄他們陣線中央,安伽斯帶了一百戰士從敵人所離開的空處,從樹林出來。

這個少年酋長向左向右搖他的手, 對他的徒衆指出敵人的所在,徒衆就分頭追趕。到了現在,戰事是分開了,胡倫人的潰散的兩翼又在樹林裏找保護, 利那披的得勝戰士們緊緊的追他們。約過一分鐘,聲音已經向各方退,在樹林中的樹枝交加所成的回響拱弧之下,逐漸聽不清楚那些聲音了。卻還有一小堆的胡倫人不肯找遮護,正在往後退,如同被窘的獅子,慢慢的,懷恨的走上斜坡,這是

Chingachgook and his band had just deserted to mingle more closely in the fray. Magua was conspicuous in this party, both by his fierce and savage mien, and by the air of haughty authority he yet maintained.

In his eagerness to expedite the pursuit, Uncas had left himself nearly alone; but the moment his eye caught the figure of Le Subtil, every other consideration was forgotten. Raising his cry of battle, which recalled some six or seven warriors, and reckless of the disparity of their numbers, he rushed upon his enemy. Le Renard, who watched the movement, paused to receive him with secret joy. But at the moment when he thought the rashness of his impetuous young assailant had left him at his mercy,[1] another shout was given, and La Longue Carabine was seen rushing to the rescue, attended by all his white associates. The Huron instantly turned, and commenced a rapid retreat up the ascent.

There was no time for greetings or congratulations; for Uncas, though unconscious of the presence of his friends, continued the pursuit with the velocity of the wind. In vain Hawkeye called to him to respect the covers; the young Mohican braved the dangerous fire of his enemies, and soon compelled them to a flight as swift as his own headlong speed. It was fortunate that the race was of short continuance, and that the white' men were much favored by their position, or the Delaware would soon have outstripped all his companions, and fallen a victim to his own temerity. But ere such a calamity could happen, the pursuers entered the Wyandot village, within striking distance of each other.

[1] at his mercy 生死由他; 任他處置.

60

末 了 的 摩 希 干 人

慶伽谷同他的手下一羣人適才所拋棄的，以便加入較爲凑近的與敵人奮鬪。那一堆人裏頭就有馬伽，從他的兇猛而野蠻的神氣，及他現在仍然維持着的驕傲威勢的態度，就看得出是他。

安伽斯因爲急於要催促追敵，幾乎剩了自己一個人在那裏；但是他一看見狡狐的形像，他就把無論什麼其他考慮全忘記了。他喊他的打仗口號，喊回來六七個戰士，他鹵莽，不顧衆寡不敵，向前直攻。狡狐留心看他的舉動，心裏私自慶幸，在那裏不動，等他來。但是一等到他以爲他的鹵莽少年仇敵在他的掌握中，又有人大聲一喊，看見『長鎗』（卽是鷹眼——譯者註。）帶着全數他的白人同袍來救。那個胡倫人立刻回過頭去，起首上斜坡快退。

這時候來不及歡迎或慶賀；因爲安伽斯雖然不曉得他的朋友們到了，還是如同狂風那樣快，接連追敵。鷹眼只管喊他不可輕視遮護；這個少年摩希干還是不管，不怕敵人的鎗，冒險進攻，不久就逼敵逃走，他們的逃走與他的輕率追趕同是一樣的快。幸而一逃一追都爲時不久，又幸而白人頗得地利，不然的話，這個狄拉維爾人不久就會遠離全數他的同袍們，變了他自己的鹵莽舉動的犧牲。但是在這樣的禍事未發現之前，追趕的人已經進了維安度村，兩方相離不過一彈之地。

THE LAST OF THE MOHICANS

Excited by the presence of their dwellings, and tired of the chase, the Hurons now made a stand, and fought around their council lodge with the fury of despair. The onset and the issue were like the passage and destruction of a whirlwind. The tomahawk of Uncas, the blows of Hawkeye, and even the still nervous arm of Munro, were all busy for that passing moment, and the ground was quickly strewed with their enemies. Still Magua, though daring and much exposed, escaped from every effort against his life, with that sort of fabled protection that was made to overlook[1] the fortunes of favored heroes in the legends of ancient poetry. Raising a yell that spoke volumes of anger and disappointment, the subtle chief, when he saw his comrades fallen, darted away from the place, attended by his two only surviving friends, leaving the Delawares engaged in stripping the dead of the bloody trophies of their victory.

But Uncas, who had vainly sought him in the *mêlée* bounded forward in pursuit; Hawkeye, Heyward, and David still pressing on his footsteps. The utmost that the scout could effect, was to keep the muzzle of his rifle a little in advance of his friend, to whom, however, it answered every purpose of a charmed shield. Once Magua appeared disposed to make another and a final effort to revenge his losses; but, abandoning his intention as soon as demonstrated, he leaped into a thicket of bushes, through which he was followed by his enemies, and suddenly entered the mouth of the cave already known to the reader. Hawkeye, who had only forborne to fire in tenderness to Uncas, raised a shout of success, and proclaimed aloud,

---

[1] overlook 忽略, 這裏剛好相反, 應解作 look over 照應.

62

末 了 的 摩 希 干 人

胡倫人看見他們自己的房屋，很為所感動，又逃跑倦乏了，現在只好黏住，在他們的會議所四圍，拼命奮鬪。衝擊與結果，如同一陣旋風的經過與毀壞。安伽斯的戰斧，鷹眼的打擊，與孟洛的仍然還是無力的手，都在那一會工夫忙於奮鬪，地下很快的鋪滿他們的仇敵。馬伽雖然大胆，雖然四面受敵，敵人無論怎樣要他的命，他都倖免，他好像得了神話所說的保護，在古時詩歌的神話裏說的，蒙神眷佑的英雄們的命運，有這樣的保護照應着。這個狡詐酋長大聲吶喊，發露許多忿怒及失望，當他看見他的同袍倒地的時候，就從那裏跳出來逃走，只有兩個生存的朋友陪伴他，任從狄拉維爾人在那裏剝奪死人的東西，作他們得勝的流血利物。

但是安伽斯在打成一團裏頭專找這個酋長，卻找不着，跳向前追趕；鷹眼，哈華特，及大衛仍然緊緊的跟隨他。探子盡他的力量所能做到的，不過是趕在他的朋友的旁邊，把鎗口向前，卻可以當作他的朋友的護身符用。馬伽有一次想再作最後的努力以雪他失敗的恥辱；但是他正要作表示的時候，又不實行，跳入一叢小樹裏頭，仇敵們穿過這裏追他，忽然走入讀者所已知的洞穴。鷹眼只因愛惜安伽斯，所以忍耐不放鎗，到了這個時候，大喊一聲，表示得勝，又大聲說，現在他們拿穩，可以捕獲他們所

that now they were certain of their game. The pursuers dashed into the long and narrow entrance, in time to catch a glimpse of the retreating forms of the Hurons. Their passage through the natural galleries and subterranean apartments of the cavern was preceded by the shrieks and cries of hundreds of women and children. The place, seen by its dim and uncertain light, appeared like the shades of the infernal regions, across which unhappy ghosts and savage demons were flitting in multitudes.

Still, Uncas kept his eye on Magua, as if life to him possessed but a single object. Heyward and the scout still pressed on his rear, actuated, though possibly in a less degree, by a common feeling. But their way was becoming intricate, in those dark and gloomy passages, and the glimpses of the retiring warriors less distinct and frequent and for a moment the trace was believed to be lost, when a white robe was seen fluttering in the further extremity of a passage that seemed to lead up the mountain.

" 'Tis Cora!" exclaimed Heyward, in a voice in which horror and delight were wildly mingled.

"Cora! Cora!" echoed Uncas, bounding forward like a deer.

" 'Tis the maiden!" shouted the scout. "Courage, lady; we come! we come!"

The chase was renewed with a diligence rendered tenfold encouraging by this glimpse of the captive. But the way was rugged, broken and in spots nearly impassable. Uncas abandoned his rifle, and leaped forward with headlong precipitation. Heyward rashly imitated his example, though both were, a moment afterward, admonished of its madness, by hearing the bellowing of a piece, that the Hurons found time to discharge down the passage in the

獵的猛獸。追趕的人們衝入長而窄的進口，剛好瞥見胡倫人們逃走。當他們走過洞裏的天然走廊及地下的隔間，前面有幾百婦孺喊叫逃走。用洞裏的暗淡而無定的光看來，這個洞穴好像黑暗地獄，有許多愁苦的死鬼及野蠻的魔鬼們從那裏成羣跳走。

安伽斯還是注意在馬伽，好像他一生惟有這一個目的物。哈華特同探子還是緊緊追隨他，兩個人都被同一感情所動，惟深淺容或不同。但是在這樣黑暗的過道裏頭，他們所走的路變作迷亂了，雖然瞥見退走的戰士們，卻看得不清楚，又隔了許久纔看見，有一會子工夫，他們相信失了敵人的蹤跡，忽然看見一條過道的較遠的盡頭處有白衣服搖動，那條過道好像是上山的路。

哈華特喊道，『那是柯爾拉！』他的聲音是混亂在一起的恐佈聲音和歡樂聲音。

安伽斯如同一隻鹿一般的向前跳，喊道，『柯爾拉！柯爾拉！』

探子大聲喊道，『是小姐；小姐呀，你放胆，我們來啦！我們來啦！』

他們瞥見這個被禁的人，就得了十倍的鼓勵，重新努力向前進。但是所走的路是很凹凸不平的，有好幾處破陷不成爲路，幾乎不能走過。安伽斯棄鎗，很鹵莽的向前跳。哈華特也鹵莽學他的榜樣，這兩個人過了俄頃，聽見一聲鎗響，他們的風狂舉動才得了警告；胡倫人有時候，向石

rocks, the bullet from which even gave the young Mohican a slight wound.

"We must close!" said the scout, passing his friend by a desperate leap; "the knaves will pick us all off at this distance; and see, they hold the maiden so as to shield themselves!"

Though his words were unheeded, or rather unheard, his example was followed by his companions, who, by incredible exertions got near enough to the fugitives to perceive that Cora was borne along between two warriors while Magua prescribed the direction and manner of their flight. At this moment the forms of all four were strongly drawn against an opening in the sky, and they disappeared. Nearly frantic with disappointment, Uncas and Heyward increased efforts that already seemed superhuman, and they issued from the cavern on the side of the mountain, in time to note the route of the pursued. The course lay up the ascent, and still continued hazardous and laborious.

Encumbered by his rifle, and, perhaps, not sustained by so deep an interest in the captive as his companions, the scout suffered the latter to precede him a little, Uncas, in his turn, taking the lead of Heyward. In this manner, rocks, precipices, and difficulties were surmounted in an incredibly short space, that at another time, and under other circumstances, would have been deemed almost insuperable. But the impetuous young men were rewarded, by finding that, encumbered with Cora, the Hurons were losing ground in the race.

"Stay, dog of the Wyandots!" exclaimed Uncas, shaking his bright tomahawk at Magua; "a Delaware girl calls stay!"

"I will go no further," cried Cora, stopping unexpectedly on a ledge of rocks, that overhung a deep precipice, at

洞的過道往下放鎗,少年摩希干受了微傷。

　　探子拚命一跳,跳過他的兩個朋友前頭,說道,『我們必要躱在一邊!那些惡棍們離我們不遠,會把我們全打死了;你們看呀,他們拿小姐作護身牌,遮護他們自己!』

　　他們雖然不聽他的話,不然邊許是聽不見他的話,他們卻學他的榜樣,這兩個人用令人不能相信的氣力,走近退走的人們,看見兩個戰士拖着柯爾拉走,馬伽吩咐他們,從什麼方向逃走,及怎樣逃走。到了這個時候陽光照着,在洞口的全數四個人的影子,就看不見了。安伽斯和哈華特大失所望,幾乎發狂,他們方才已經是超人的努力了,現在更加努力,從山邊洞口跑出來,剛好還有時候看見被追趕的人們所走的路徑。逃走的方向還是上山,仍然是危險的,辛苦的。

　　探子被他的鎗所累,也許他對於被獲的姑娘不如他的同伴們關切到那樣深,他就讓他們相離不甚遠的在他的前頭走,安伽斯卻走在哈華特之前。他們就是這樣走過許多石頭,峭壁,在令人不能相信那樣短的時間,推倒種種爲難,若在別的時候,處別的環境,他們就許以爲這樣的爲難,是幾乎不能推倒的。但是勇猛的少年們,看見胡倫人被柯爾拉所拖累,走得慢,快被敵人趕上,就得了他們努力的獎賞。

　　安伽斯對馬伽搖動他的發亮的戰斧,喊道,『維安度的狗,站着,一個狄拉維爾女子喊站着!』

　　離山頂不遠有一個很陡的懸崖,柯爾拉出其不意的坐在懸崖的一塊突出的石頭上,喊道,『我再不往前走了。

no great distance from the summit of the mountain. "Kill me if thou wilt, detestable Huron; I will go no further."

The supporters of the maiden raised their ready tomahawks with the impious joy that fiends are thought to take in mischief, but Magua stayed their uplifted arms. The Huron chief, after casting the weapons he had wrested from his companions over the rock, drew his knife, and turned to his captive, with a look in which conflicting passions fiercely contended.

"Woman," he said, "choose; the wigwam or the knife of Le Subtil!"

Cora regarded him not, but dropping on her knees, she raised her eyes and stretched her arms toward heaven, saying, in a meek and yet confiding voice:—

"I am Thine! do with me as Thou seest best!"

"Woman," repeated Magua, hoarsely, and endeavoring in vain to catch a glance from her serene and beaming eye, "choose!"

But Cora neither heard nor heeded his demand. The form of the Huron trembled in every fibre, and he raised his arm on high, but dropped it again with a bewildered air, like one who doubted. Once more he struggled with himself and lifted the keen weapon again; but just then a piercing cry was heard above them, and Uncas appeared leaping frantically, from a fearful height, upon the ledge. Magua recoiled a step; and one of his assistants, profiting by the chance, sheathed his own knife in the bosom of Cora.

The Huron sprang like a tiger on his offending and already retreating countryman, but the falling form of Uncas separated the unnatural combatants. Diverted from his object by his interruption, and maddened by the murder he had just witnessed, Magua buried his weapon in the back of the prostrate Delaware, uttering an

你這個可恨的胡倫人，你若要殺我，只管動手，我是不肯再往前走的了。』

據說惡鬼是好樂禍的，參扶柯爾拉的兩個人正在很高興的舉斧要打死她，馬伽卻擋住他們已經舉起的手。這個胡倫酋長，把他所奪的斧子在山石上摔往山下，拔出刀來，對着柯爾拉說話，他的神色表示他的互相衝突的激情，在那裏奮闘。

他說道，『女子，你還是願意到狡狐的家裏，抑或願意吃刀子，請你自擇！』

柯爾拉不理他，雙膝跪在地下，舉目及伸手向天，用一種婉順及深信的聲音，說道：——

『上帝，我是你的人，你最喜歡怎樣處置我，就怎樣處置我。』

馬伽正在嘗試要她的鎭靜的及發光的眼看一看他，她不肯看他，他聲音沙沙的又說道，『女人，你擇呀！』

柯爾拉旣不聽見，亦不理他的號令。這個胡倫人渾身發抖，高舉他的手，他帶着迷亂無主的神色，把手又垂下來，好像遲疑不決的。他又同自己奮闘一次，又把利刀舉起來；這時候他聽見頭上有人刺耳的大喊，原來是安伽斯從可怕那樣高的地方，如發狂的，跳在突出的石頭上。馬伽退後一步；他的一個幫手利用這個機會，一刀刺入柯爾拉的胸膛。

這個胡倫人如老虎一般，撲他的得罪了他卻已經退走的同族，但是有墜下來的安伽斯分開這兩個不自然的相闘人。馬伽被阻，不能達目的，又被剛才他所看見的刺殺所激怒，變作瘋狂了，就把他的刀子刺入倒地的安伽斯

unearthly shout as he committed the dastardly deed. But Uncas arose from the blow, as the wounded panther turns upon his foe, and struck the murderer of Cora to his feet, by an effort in which the last of his failing strength was expended. Then with a stern and steady look, he turned to Le Subtil, and indicated, by the expression of his eye, all that he would do, had not the power deserted him. The latter seized the nerveless arm of the unresisting Delaware, and passed his knife into his bosom three several times, before his victim, still keeping his gaze riveted on his enemy, with a look of inextinguishable scorn, fell dead at his feet.

"Mercy! mercy! Huron," cried Heyward, from above, in tones nearly choked by horror; "give mercy, and thou shalt receive it!"

Whirling the bloody knife up at the imploring youth, the victorious Magua uttered a cry so fierce, so wild, and yet so joyous, that it conveyed the sounds of savage triumph to the ears of those who fought in the valley, a thousand feet below. He was answered by a burst from the lips of the scout, whose tall person was just then seen moving swiftly toward him, along those dangerous crags, with steps as bold and reckless as if he possessed the power to move in air. But when the hunter reached the scene of the ruthless massacre, the ledge was tenanted only by the dead.

His keen eye took a single look at the victims, and then shot its glances over the difficulties of the ascent in his front. A form stood at the brow of the mountain, on the very edge of the giddy height, with uplifted arms, in an awful attitude of menace. Without stopping to consider his person, the rifle of Hawkeye was raised; but a rock,

的背，當他做這樣卑劣無勇人所做的事時，他大喊一聲，好像是鬼叫一般。但是安伽斯受了一刺，爬起來，這條受傷的虎掉轉身來，對着他的仇敵，打殺那個殺害柯爾拉的兇手，打倒在地，他這一努力，把他的最後的薄弱氣力全用盡了。他隨卽帶着一副嚴厲鎮定神色，對着狡狐，用眼色表示，假使他不是氣力消耗淨盡，他會怎樣對付他。馬伽抓住不抵抗的安伽斯的無知覺的手，用刀刺入他的胸膛好幾次，他的犧牲才死，倒在他脚下，死者的眼直瞪着他的仇人，帶着不能熄滅的藐視神色。

哈華特從高處喊，他的聲音幾乎被他所眼見的慘事所閉塞，他喊道，『胡倫人，慈悲呀！慈悲呀！你給人以慈悲，人亦給你以慈悲！』

得勝的馬伽，把鮮血淋漓的刀向上摔這個求饒的少年，大喊一聲，又兇，又野，卻帶着得意腔調，在一千尺山谷底下打仗的人們都聽見這樣得意的野蠻聲音。探子說兩句話答他，探子的高大身軀正在快快的向他這裏來，沿着陡懸的巖石走，他大胆鹵莽的踏步，好像他有本事能在空中走動一般。但是等到這個獵者（指鷹眼——譯者註。）走到慘殺的地點，懸崖上只有被殺的人。

他的利眼只看一看兩個被殺的人，隨卽看了好幾眼在他面前登山的山坡的許多爲難。有一個人站在山頂，站在令人見了發暈的邊上，高舉兩手，作嚇人的狀態。鷹眼這時候不顧自身就舉鎗；但是有一塊石頭墜在山下的一

which fell on the head of one of the fugitives below, exposed the indignant and glowing countenance of the honest Gamut. Then Magua issued from a crevice, and stepping with calm indifference over the body of the last of his associates, he leaped a wide fissure, and ascended the rocks at a point where the arm of David could not reach him. A single bound would carry him to the brow of the precipice, and assure his safety. Before taking the leap, however, the Huron paused, and shaking his hand at the scout, he shouted:—

"The pale faces are dogs! the Delawares, women! Magua leaves them on the rocks, for the crows!"

Laughing hoarsely, he made a desperate leap, and fell short of his mark; though his hands grasped a shrub on the verge of the height The form of Hawkeye had crouched like a beast about to take its spring, and his frame trembled so violently with eagerness, that the muzzle of the half-raised rifle played like a leaf fluttering in the wind. Without exhausting himself with fruitless efforts, the cunning Magua suffered his body to drop to the length of his arms, and found a fragment for his feet to rest on. Then summoning all his powers, he renewed the attempt, and so far succeeded as to draw his knees on the edge of the mountain. It was now, when the body of his enemy was most collected together, that the agitated weapon of the scout was drawn to his shoulder. The surrounding rocks themselves were not steadier than the piece became for the single instant that it poured out its contents. The arms of the Huron relaxed, and his body fell back a little, while his knees still kept their position. Turning a relentless look on his enemy, he shook a hand in grim defiance. But his hold loosened, and his dark person was seen cutting

末 了 的 摩 希 干 人

個逃人的頭上，露出老實的伽末特（即大衛——譯者註。）的憤怒的及冒火的面目。馬伽隨卽從山罅出來，冷淡鎮靜的踏步在他最後的同袍的屍身上邁進，跳過一條寬澗，走上山石，大衛的手夠不着他。他只要一跳就到了懸崖上，就很安穩了。這個胡倫卻在將跳之前停頓一會兒，對着探子揮拳，大聲喊道；——

『白人是狗！狄拉維爾人是女人！馬伽留他們在山石上餒烏鴉！』

他沙聲大笑，拚命一跳，跳不到他所想跳到的地點；卻用兩手抓住高崖邊的一堆小樹。鷹眼蹲着身子，好像一隻野獸快要跳的狀態，他着急到渾身很利害的發抖，那半舉的鎗口抖動，如同一片樹葉在風裏搖動。那個狡狐的馬伽不肯費無用的力，徒耗自己的氣力，讓他的身體向下墜，墜到有兩臂長得那樣遠，找着石塊作立足地。他於是出盡全力，嘗試再往下墜，居然能夠提起兩膝緊靠山邊。到了這個時候，探子的仇敵的身體最團聚在一處，探子把發抖的鎗緊靠他的肩。當放鎗的一刹那間，那支鎗穩定不動，如同四面的山石。馬伽的兩臂鬆了，他的身體向後稍墜，兩膝還是不動。他舉目看他的仇人，毫無悔禍神色，還搖一手，表示一種很難看的不甘罷手的意思。但是他的兩手鬆了，只看見他的黑身子頭向下，凌空下墜，俄頃間就

the air with its head downward, for a fleeting instant, until it glided past the fringe of shrubbery which clung to the mountain, in its rapid flight to destruction.

CHAPTER XXXIII

"They fought like brave men, long and well,
  They piled that ground with Moslem slain,
They conquered—but Bozzaris fell,
  Bleeding at every vein.
His few surviving comrades say
His smile when rang their proud hurrah,
  And the red field was won;
Then saw in death his eyelids close
Calmly, as to a night's repose,
  Like flowers at set of sun."

—HALLECK

Six Delaware girls, with their long, dark, flowing tresses falling loosely across their bosoms, stood apart, and only gave proofs of their existence as they occasionally strewed sweet-scented herbs and forest flowers on a litter of fragrant plants, that, under a pall of Indian robes, supported all that now remained of the ardent, high-souled, and generous Cora. Her form was concealed in many wrappers of the same simple manufacture, and her face was shut forever from the gaze of men. At her feet was seated the desolate Munro. His aged head was bowed nearly to the earth, in compelled submission to the stroke of Providence; but a hidden anguish struggled about his furrowed brow, that was only partially concealed by the careless locks of gray that had fallen, neglected, on his temples. Gamut stood at his side, his meek head bared to the rays of the sun, while his eyes, wandering and concerned,[1] seemed to

---

[1] concerned 憫憂; 憂愁; 關切.

74

看不見了，隨後向殺身的地方下墜得很快，在山邊的一堆小樹林邊上溜過。

第三十三回　　土人的葬儀

有六個狄拉維爾女子披着長且黑的鬆頭髮，垂在她們胸口，另外站在一處，當她們有時鋪香草和樹林裏的花在一床的香樹上，才看見她們；這張床有幾件印度袍子作柩衣，裝着熱烈激昂及性情慷慨的柯爾拉的遺骸。她的全身有好幾層同樣的單簡袍服包裹住，人們永遠看不見她的面了。那個孤寒的孟洛坐在她脚下。他低垂他的年老的頭，幾乎垂到地，不得不服從上天的打擊；但是在他的兩眉縐紋之間，可以看見有一種深藏不露的痛心在那裏奮鬪，只是多少被不曾梳理的垂在他的兩邊太陽的白髮所遮掩。伽末特站在他旁邊，他的溫和的頭不戴帽子，有陽光照着，當下他的兩眼，露出憂愁神色，四圍的看，好像是

be equally divided between that little volume, which contained so many quaint but holy maxims, and the being in whose behalf his soul yearned to administer consolation. Heyward was also nigh, supporting himself against a tree and endeavoring to keep down those sudden risings of sorrow that it required his utmost manhood to subdue.

But sad and melancholy as this group may easily be imagined, it was far less touching than another that occupied the opposite space of the same area. Seated, as in life, with his form and limbs arranged in grave and decent composure, Uncas appeared, arrayed in the most gorgeous ornaments that the wealth of the tribe could furnish. Rich plumes nodded above his head; wampum, gorgets, bracelets, and medals adorned his person in profusion; though his dull eye and vacant lineaments too strongly contradicted the idle tale of pride they would convey.

Directly in front of the corpse Chingachgook was placed, without arms, paint, or adornment of any sort, except the bright blue blazonry of his race, that was indelibly impressed on his naked bosom. During the long period that the tribe had been thus collected, the Mohican warrior had kept a steady, anxious look on the cold and senseless countenance of his son. So riveted and intense had been that gaze, and so changeless his attitude, that a stranger might not have told the living from the dead, but for the occasional gleamings of a troubled spirit, that shot athwart the dark visage of one, and the death-like calm that had forever settled on the lineaments of the other.

The scout was hard by, leaning in a pensive posture on his own fatal and avenging weapon; while Tamenund, supported by the elders of his nation, occupied a high place at hand, whence he might look down on the mute and sorrowful assemblage of his people.

末 了 的 摩 希 干 人

平均分開，注意於兩件事，注意於那本小書，內裏有許多古老而是神聖的格言，又注意於死者，他的靈魂爲死者起見，渴想施以安慰。（作者好用區別字，於此可見——譯者註。）哈華特也站近那裏，靠着一株樹，努力要壓下忽然發生的憂戚，卻要用盡男子漢的氣概才壓得下來，不作兒女態。

我們可以容易想像這幾個人的憂愁情狀，但是遠不如在對面的情景那樣動人。對面放着安伽斯的屍身，如生時一樣坐着，肢體安放得嚴肅整齊，穿了本部的財富所能供給的最華麗服飾。頭上插了富麗的鳥羽，滿身披掛螺鈿帶子，護身甲，鐲子，寶星；可惜他的無光的眼，無神的容貌，同這許多服飾所表示的無謂的高傲，太過相反了。

慶伽谷坐在死屍之前，他不執兵器，不塗臉，又無任何裝飾品，只有他本族的亮藍徽章，刺在他的胸脯，這是不能消滅的。當費了許多時候召集本部落的人眾時，這個摩希干酋長兩眼專心的及着急的注視他的兒子的冷而無知覺的面。他的注視是專一的，如同釘在兒子的臉上，他的狀態始終不改變，若是一個生人走來，很許辨不出來那一個是死的，那一個是活的，只有看見這一個有時從他的黑臉放出他的受了煩惱的精神的眼光來，才曉得他是活的，在那一個的臉上，有永遠在那裏的死人的寂靜，才曉得他是死的。

探子站得與屍很近，靠着他的能致命及能報仇的兵器，作深念的狀態；塔米能（Tamenund 土人的神父或主教——譯者註。）有他本族的幾個長老參扶着，坐在不遠的高座，他從這個地方，可以居高臨下的，看他的緘默懷戀的聚集在這裏的人眾。

77

THE LAST OF THE MOHICANS

Just within the inner edge of the circle stood a soldier, in the military attire of a strange nation; and without it was his war-horse, in the center of a collection of mounted domestics, seemingly in readiness to undertake some distant journey. The vestments of the stranger announced him to be one who held a responsible situation near the person of the captain of the Canadas; and who, as it would now seem, finding his errand of peace frustrated by the fierce impetuosity of his allies, was content to become a silent and sad spectator of the fruits of a contest that he had arrived too late to anticipate.

The day was drawing to the close of its first quarter, and yet had the multitude maintained its breathing stillness since its dawn. No sound louder than a stifled sob had been heard among them, nor had even a limb moved throughout that long and painful period, except to perform the simple and touching offerings that were made, from time to time, in commemoration of the dead. The patience and forbearance of Indian fortitude could alone support such an appearance of abstraction, as seemed now to have turned each dark and motionless figure into stone.

At length, the sage of the Delawares stretched forth an arm, and leaning on the shoulders of his attendants, he arose with an air as feeble as if another age had already intervened between the man who had met his nation the preceding day, and him who now tottered on his elevated stand.

"Men of the Lenape!" he siad, in hollow tones, that sounded like a voice charged with some prophetic mission: "the face of the Manitou is behind a cloud! His eye is turned from you; His ears are shut; His tongue gives no answer. You see Him not; yet His judgments are before

末 了 的 摩 希 干 人

　　正在圈子的裏邊，站着一個兵，穿了一個外路民族的軍裝；在圈子外站着他的戰馬，在一羣騎馬僕從中央，好像要預備遠行。這個外路人的裝束，表示他是在加拿大族的頭目左右的一個負責的人；從現時看來，這個人見得他的議和使命被他同盟們的激烈的衝動所破壞，只好作一個不發言的及愁苦的旁觀人，看兩族相爭的結果，可惜他來得太遲，不能預先阻止這樣的競爭。

　　自破曉到現在已經有幾點鐘了，羣衆還是屏息不響。最多不過聽見哭不出聲的嗚咽，過了這許久及痛苦的時候，無人動手或動脚，只有隨時作單簡而動人的供獻；以紀念死者。只有印度人的毅力的堅忍能夠受得住這樣的不言不動的沉寂，現在好像把每個不動的黑人變作石人了。

　　後來狄拉維爾人的聖人伸出一隻手，扶住他的隨從們的肩膀，站起來，帶着極其衰弱的神色，好像前天來會他的民族的人同今天在高座上站立不穩的人，已經隔了一世。

　　他用好像有預言使命的深沉腔調說道，『利那披人呀！曼尼圖（Manitou 北美印度人的神——譯者註。）被一片雲遮住了！他的眼掉過去不看你們；他的兩耳是塞住了；他的舌頭不答話。你們不見他：但是他的判斷還在你

you. Let your hearts be open and your spirits tell no lie. Men of the Lenape! the face of the Manitou is behind a cloud."

As this simple and yet terrible annunciation stole on the ears of the multitude, a stillness as deep and awful succeeded as if the venerated spirit they worshipped had uttered the words without the aid of human organs; and even the inanimate Uncas appeared a being of life, compared with the humbled and submissive throng by whom he was surrounded. As the immediate effect, however, gradually passed away, a low murmur of voices commenced a sort of chant in honor of the dead. The sounds were those of females, and were thrillingly soft and wailing. The words were connected by no regular continuation, but as one ceased another took up the eulogy, or lamentation, whichever it might be called, and gave vent to her emotions in such language as was suggested by her feelings and the occasion. At intervals the speaker was interrupted by general and loud bursts of sorrow, during which the girls around the bier of Cora plucked the plants and flowers blindly from her body, as if bewildered with grief. But, in the milder moments of their plaint, these emblems of purity and sweetness were cast back to their places, with every sign of tenderness and regret. . . . .

A girl, selected for the task by her rank and qualifications, commenced by modest allusions to the qualities of the deceased warrior, embellishing her expressions with those oriental images that the Indians have probably brought with them from the extremes of the other continent, and which form of themselves a link to connect the ancient histories of the two worlds. She called him the "panther of his tribe;" and described him as one whose moccasin left

末 了 的 摩 希 干 人

們面前。你們要開心見誠，不要說謊。利那披人呀！曼尼圖的臉在一片雲的後面。』

　　當這樣單簡而可怕的宣言，偷入羣衆的耳朵的時候，繼以不響不動，其深沉與可怕，好像他們的禮拜的神靈，親自說話，並非借助於人類的口舌；拿包圍安伽斯的受抑屈的與甘心服從的羣衆與死了的安伽斯相比，好像安伽斯還是個活人。但當立刻發現的效果逐漸過去了的時候，一種低微的喃喃聲音，起首唱歌，追悼死者。聲音是女人的，柔和而哀傷，聲音很尖。字句並無循序接續的聯綴，一句完了，又接上一句，或是讚美的話，或是哀悼的話，照着各人的感情，及這次的喪事所激發的各人的情緒。有幾次相隔不久，衆人大聲痛哭，阻住宣言人說話，那時候包圍柯爾拉棺架的女子們好像是悲痛到迷亂了，亂從她身上摘取花木。但是當她們的悲痛較爲和平的時候，又把表示清潔及温柔的花木，放回原處，帶着種種慈愛及婉惜的表示。

　　於是挑選一個階級與資格合宜的女子作說話人，她就起首用謙抑話表揚已死的戰士的德性，用東方的比喻話，裝飾她的話語，這些比喻話也許是從另一大洲的極端地方帶來的，這就成爲一個連環，聯合兩個世界的荒古歷史。她說他是『她的部落的老虎；』她說他的鹿皮鞋在露上

81

no trail on the dews; whose bound was like the leap of a young fawn; whose eye was brighter than a star in the dark night; and whose voice, in battle, was loud as the thunder of the Manitou. She reminded him of the mother who bore him, and dwelt forcibly on the happiness she must feel in possessing such a son. She bade him tell her, when they met in the world of spirits, that the Delaware girls had shed tears above the grave of her child, and had called her blessed.

Then, they who succeeded, changing their tones to a milder and still more tender strain, alluded, with the delicacy and sensitiveness of women, to the stranger maiden, who had left the upper earth at a time so near his own departure as to render the will of the Great Spirit too manifest to be disregarded. They admonished him to be kind to her, and to have consideration for her ignorance of those arts which were so necessary to the comfort of a warrior like himself. They dwelt upon her matchless beauty, and on her noble resolution, without the taint of envy and as angels may be thought to delight in a superior excellence; adding, that these endowments should prove more than equivalent for any little imperfections in her education.

After which, others again, in due succession, spoke to the maiden herself, in the low, soft language of tenderness and love. They exhorted her to be of cheerful mind, and to fear nothing for her future welfare. A hunter would be her companion, who knew how to provide for her smallest wants; and a warrior was at her side who was able to protect her against every danger. They promised that her path should be pleasant, and her burden light. They cautioned her against unavailing regrets for the friends of her

末 了 的 摩 希 干 人

不留痕跡；他的跳如同一條小鹿的跳，他的眼比黑夜的星還要亮；他打仗的聲音與曼尼圖的雷聲一樣響。她請他記得生他的母親，力說她有了這樣的一個兒子，必定是歡樂的。她請他當他們母子在鬼神的世界相見時告訴他的母親，說狄拉維爾的女子們，曾在她的兒子墳上滴淚，稱她是有福人。

隨後上來的人們，改變她們的腔調，改作更溫柔，用女人的細心措辭，感覺靈敏的說話，說到這個外國女子，說她離開在上的世界時，同他離開的時候很相近，就顯然見得大神靈的意思是不能不顧的。她們勸他以慈愛待她，要一個如他這樣的戰士安樂，必要做許多事，她卻不曉得做，她們勸他原諒她。她們稱讚她的無可與比的美貌，及她的高貴的剛決，無絲毫妒忌如同安琪兒，她們想安琪兒們大約是以一種更高的美德爲樂；她們還說她既有這許多天賦的美德，就不止抵得過她的教育的缺點。

此後又有別的人按序上來，用溫柔及親愛的低聲及柔和說話，對已死的女子說。她們力勸她存着快樂的心境，不要害怕她將來的幸福。一個獵人做她的同伴，他曉得怎樣供給她的最小的需要；在她身邊的可是一個戰士，他能夠保護她，以抗拒無論什麼危險。她們相信她所走的路是可以使她娛悅的，她的擔負是輕的。她們警告她不要捨不得她少年時的朋友們，捨不得也是無用的，勸她不要

THE LAST OF THE MOHICANS

youth, and the scenes where her fathers had dwelt; assuring her that the "blessed[1] hunting-grounds of the Lenape" contained vales as pleasant, streams as pure, and flowers as sweet, as the "heaven of the pale faces." They advised her to be attentive to the wants of her companion, and never to forget the distinction which the Manitou had so wisely established between them. Then, in a wild burst of their chant, they sang with united voices the temper of the Mohican's mind. They pronounced him noble, manly, and generous; all that became a warrior, and all that a maid might love. Clothing their ideas in the most remote and subtle images, they betrayed, that, in the short period of their intercourse, they had discovered, with the intuitive perception of their sex, the truant[2] disposition of his inclinations. The Delaware girls had found no favor in his eyes! He was of a race that had once been lords on the shores of the salt lake, and his wishes had led him back to a people who dwelt about the graves of his fathers. Why should not such a predilection[3] be encouraged! That she was of blood purer and richer than the rest of her nation, and eye might have seen; that she was equal to the dangers and daring of a life in the woods, her conduct had proved; and now, they added, the "wise one of the earth" had transplanted her to a place where she would find congenial spirits, and might be forever happy.

Then, with another transition in voice and subject, allusions were made to the virgin who wept in the adjacent lodge. They compared her to flakes of snow; as pure, as white, as brilliant, and as liable to melt in the fierce heats

---

[1] blessed 荷天賜福的. [2] truant 逃學; 失約; 溺職. [3] predilection 嗜好; 偏好.

捨不得她的祖先們所住的地方；她們勸她深信利那披族的荷天賜福的圍場也有娛人的山谷，清潔的溪流，及香花，如同『白人的天堂』所有的一樣。她們勸她對於她的同伴的需要，要小心在意，永遠不要忘記曼尼圖所明智分開的夫婦之別。她們於是同聲狂歌，頌揚這個摩希干人的心性。她們說他名貴，有丈夫氣概，又慷慨；凡是一個戰士所應有的美德，他無不有，凡是一個女子所愛於男的好處，他亦無不有。她們用最不倫不類及最奧妙的比喻，以裝飾她們的意思，她們微露其意，說她們與他相處不久，她們以女人的本有的感覺，窺見他的性情的溺職的傾向。（殆指安伽斯不愛本族女子——譯者註。）原來狄拉維爾的女子們不值他一顧！他原是貴族的子孫，有一度曾經做過鹹湖邊土地的君主，他的想望引他回想在他的祖墳左右居住的一個民族。這樣的一種偏好爲什麼就不該鼓勵！無論什麼人都可以看得出她的血比她本國其餘的人更清更富；她的行爲又曾證明她能夠對付在樹林過生活的危險；她們又說『世上的聖人』現時把她移到一個地方，她在那裏得着一個與她性情相近的人，可以永遠歡樂了。

　　隨後改變了聲音及題目，說到在隣近房子裏啼哭的女子。（大約是安伽斯的未婚妻——譯者註。）她們比她作雪花；同雪花一樣的清潔，一樣的白，一樣的有光彩，一樣的容易被夏天的炎熱所溶化，一樣易於被冬天的嚴寒所

of summer, or congeal in the frosts of winter. They doubted not that she was lovely in the eyes of the young chief, whose skin and whose sorrow seemed so like her own; but, though far from expressing such a preference; it was evident they deemed her less excellent than the maid they mourned. Still they denied her no meed her rare charms might properly claim. Her ringlets were compared to the exuberant tendrils of the vine, her eye to the blue vault of the heavens, and the most spotless cloud, with its glowing flush of the sun, was admitted to be less attractive than her bloom.

During these and similar songs nothing was audible but the murmurs of the music; relieved, as it was, or rather rendered terrible, by those occasional bursts of grief which might be called its choruses. The Delawares themselves listened like charmed men; and it was very apparent, by the variations of their speaking countenances,[1] how deep and true was their sympathy. Even David was not reluctant to lend his ears to the tones of voices so sweet; and long ere the chant was ended, his gaze announced that his soul was enthralled.

The scout, to whom alone, of all the white men, the words were intelligible, suffered himself to be a little aroused from the meditative posture, and bent his face aside, to catch their meanings, as the girls proceeded. But when they spoke of the future prospects of Cora and Uncas, he shook his head, like one who knew the error of their simple creed,[2] and resuming his reclining attitude, he maintained it until the ceremony, if that might be called a

---

[1] speaking countenances 表情的神色. [2] creed 宗教的信條; 所信的道理; 見解.

疑結。她們相信從這個少年酋長眼中看來,她是一個可愛
的女子,他的皮色及愁苦與她的相同,她們雖然絕不肯說
出另一個女子更好, 她們顯然以為她不如她們所追悼的
那個女子好。雖是這樣說,她們仍然還她以她的罕見的美
貌可以正當得着的稱讚。她們以葡萄的豐盛的蔓鬚比她
的鬈髮,以天青色比她的眼, 她們還承認,帶着日光的最
清白的雲,還不如她的鮮豔容貌那樣引人。

　　當她們唱這樣的歌及同類的歌的時候, 惟聽見喃喃
的音樂,並不聽見其他聲音; 有時衝出一陣陣慘哭聲音,
可以稱為和歌,減輕喪歌的慘痛,或使其變作可怕。狄拉
維爾人自己也在那裏細聽,如同受迷的人;從他們的表情
神色看來,他們所表的同情顯然是深的,是真的。大衛也
願意聽這樣好聽的腔調;遠在她們尚未唱完之先,他的眼
神表示他的靈魂受了束縛。

　　在全數在場的白人裏頭,惟有探子懂得她們的話,他
本來在那裏獨自深念,聽了土人的喪歌, 多少提起精神,
歪着頭,聽她們說什麼。但是當她們說到柯爾拉及安伽斯
的將來光景的時候,他卻搖頭,好像曉得她們的單簡見解
是錯的,隨後還是斜着身子,一直等到行完禮, 倘若這樣

ceremony, in which feeling was so deeply imbued, was finished. Happily for the self-command of both Heyward and Munro, they knew not the meaning of the wild sounds they heard.

Chingachgook was a solitary exception to the interest manifested by the native part of the audience. His look never changed throughout the whole of the scene, nor did a muscle move in his rigid countenance, even at the wildest or the most pathetic parts of the lamentation. The cold and senseless remains of his son was all to him, and every other sense but that of sight seemed frozen, in order that his eyes might take their final gaze at those lineaments he had so long loved, and which were now about to be closed forever from his view."

In this stage of the funeral obsequies, a warrior much renowned for deeds in arms, and more especially for services in the recent combat, a man of stern and grave demeanor, advanced slowly from the crowd, and placed himself nigh the person of the dead.

"Why hast thou left us, pride of the Wapanachki?" he said, addressing himself to the dull ears of Uncas, as if the empty clay retained the faculties of the animated man. "Thy time has been like that of the sun when in the trees; thy glory brighter than his light at noonday. Thou art gone, youthful warrior, but a hundréd Wyandots are clearing the briers from thy path to the world of spirits. Who that saw thee in battle would believe that thou couldst die? Who before thee has ever shown Uttawa the way into the fight? Thy feet were like the wings of eagles; thine arm heavier than falling branches from the pine; and thy voice like the Manitou when he speaks in the clouds. The tongue of Uttawa is weak," he added, looking

末 了 的 靡 希 干 人

令人發生深情的舉動，可以叫做禮。好在哈華特及孟洛兩個人不懂得他們所聽見的野人聲音說的是什麼，不致激動他們的情緒。

在場的士人們無不動情，惟有慶伽谷獨不然。自始至終他絕不改變他的神色，卽使她們悲歌到極無節制及極能感動人的部分時候，他還是板着面孔，動也不動。他的全數官覺都變作凝凍的了，只有視官不曾變，全注在他的兒子的冷的及無知覺的屍骸，使他的兩眼可以對於他所親愛甚久的面貌，作最後的注視，現時快要蓋棺，他永遠再看不見了。

殯葬的禮節行到這個地步，就有一個以善戰聞名的戰士，尤其以新近的戰功顯著的戰士，是一個儀表嚴肅的人，從人羣裏頭慢慢走上前，站在與死人相近的地方。

他對着安伽斯的聽不見的兩耳說話，好像這樣無了靈魂的泥士還保存生人的能力一般，他說道，『倭柏那琪（Wapanachki 又是這一族人的別稱——譯者註。）的驕子呀，你為什麼棄我們走了？你正在日在樹上的盛年；你的光榮比中午的陽光還亮。少年戰士，你是去了，但是有一百個維安度人替你開道，斬除荆棘，以便你前往鬼神的世界。凡是看見你打仗的人，誰肯相信你是可以死的？在你之先，那裏有人教烏打和（Uttawa）怎樣臨陣打仗呀？你的兩足如同鷹的兩翼；你的手臂重過杉樹墜下來的樹枝；你的聲音如同曼尼圖在雲端說話』。他帶着一種愁慘

about him with a melancholy gaze, "and his heart exceeding heavy. Pride of the Wapanachki, why hast thou left us?"

He was succeeded by others, in due order, until most of the high and gifted men of the nation had sung or spoken their tribute of praise over the names of the deceased chief. When each had ended, another deep and breathing silence reigned in all the place.

Then a low, deep sound was heard, like the suppressed accompaniment of distant music, rising just high enough on the air to be audible, and yet so indistinctly, as to leave its character, and the place whence it proceeded, alike matters of conjecture. It was, however, succeeded by another and another strain, each in a higher key, until they grew on the ear, first in long drawn and often repeated interjections, and finally in words. The lips of Chingachgook had so far parted, as to announce that it was the monody of the father. Though not an eye was turned toward him, nor the smallest sign of impatience exhibited, it was apparent, by the manner in which the multitude elevated their heads to listen, that they drank in the sounds with an intentness of attention that none but Tamenund himself had ever before commanded. But they listened in vain. The strains rose just so loud as to become intelligible, and then grew fainter and more trembling, until they finally sank on the ear, as if borne away by a passing breath of wind. The lips of the Sagamore closed, and he remained silent in his seat, looking, with his riveted eye and motionless form, like some creature that had been turned from the Almighty hand with the form but without the spirit of a man. The Delawares, who knew by these symptoms that the mind of their friend was not prepared

的眼色，四圍看看，又說道，『烏打和的舌頭無力，他的心極其沉痛。倭柏那琪的驕子呀，你為什麼捨我們而去？』

他說完了，還有好幾個人按着次序上來說話，等到本部族裏頭大多數的高貴的及善於辭令的人們對已死的酋長，或歌唱過，或演說過他們所貢獻的讚美話。每人說過之後，又有一會兒的深沉及只有喘息的寂靜。

隨後聽見一片低微而深沉的聲音，好像是遠處音樂的壓下來的絃管聲，起在空中，高到剛可以聽見，卻聽得不甚清楚，令人猜不着究竟是什麼聲音，是從那裏來的。隨後又是一陣一陣的聲音相繼，調子越高，初時聽得不過是拉長的及屢次複說的嗟歎聲，最後卻是字句。慶伽谷的兩唇分開，這就表示是這個父親的輓歌。雖然並無一人看他，雖然無人流露極輕微的不耐煩，衆人都抬頭細聽，這就顯然見得他們極其專心致志的聽這種聲音，從前只有塔米能自己曾使他們這樣專心致志。他們只管留心聽，亦是枉然。那一派聲音響到剛可以聽見，隨後越變越低，又越變作抖抖的聲音，後來聽不見了，好像一陣風經過，把聲音吹走了。酋長閉着兩唇，坐在那裏不響，身子不動，眼睛釘着的看，好像是上帝手造的一種人，只賦以人形，並未賦以人的精靈。狄拉維爾人由這樣的徵象曉得他們的

for so mighty an effort of fortitude, relaxed in their attention; and, with an innate delicacy, seemed to bestow all their thoughts on the obsequies of the stranger maiden.

A signal was given, by one of their elder chiefs, to the women, who crowded that part of the circle near which the body of Cora lay. Obedient to the sign, the girls raised the bier to the elevation of their heads, and advanced with slow and regulated steps, chanting, as they proceeded, another wailing song in praise of the deceased. Gamut, who had been a close observer of rites he deemed so heathenish, now bent his head over the shoulder of the unconscious father, whispering:—

"They move with the remains of thy child; shall we not follow, and see them interred with Christian burial?"

Munro started, as if the last trumpet had sounded in his ear, and bestowing one anxious and hurried glance around him, he arose and followed in the simple train, with the mien of a soldier,[1] but bearing the full burden of a parent's suffering. His friends pressed around him wth a sorrow, that was too strong to be termed sympathy—even the young Frenchman joined in the procession, with the air of a man who was sensibly touched at the early and melancholy fate of one so lovely. But when the last and humblest female of the tribe had joined in the wild, and yet ordered array, the men of the Lenape contracted their circle, and formed again around the person of Uncas, as silent, as grave, and as motionless as before.

The place which had been chosen for the grave of Cora was a little knoll, where a cluster of young and beautiful pines had taken root, forming of themselves a melancholy

---

[1] with the mien of a soldier 反 說 就 是 不 作 兒 女 子 態 度.

末 了 的 摩 希 干 人

朋友的心力不曾預備支持這樣的大毅力，就不那樣注意，他們有一種天生的精細，好像把他們全數的思想移在那個外國女子的殯儀上。

於是有一個年長的酋長作手勢，示意於聚在與柯爾拉遺骸相近的地方的一羣女人。這些女子們服從他的命令，把屍架抬起來，高與她們的頭齊，用整齊的脚步，慢慢向前走，一面唱另一輓歌以稱讚死者。伽末特很留心觀察他以爲是異教人的禮節，現在低頭在那個無知覺的父親肩膀上附耳說道；——

『她們抬走你的女兒的遺骸；我們還不跟她們走，看着她們用基督教儀節安葬麼？』

孟洛一驚，好像最後的喇叭在他的耳朵裏吹，匆匆的，着急的，四圍一看，站起來，跟着這一羣人走，帶着軍人的態度，卻擔負一個爲人父的全數慘痛。他的朋友們都走上前，在四面湊近他，表示憂戚，他們都很悲痛的，不能說是憐憫——連那個少年法蘭西人也加入跟着走，他的神色表示對於這個美貌女子死得這樣慘，死得這樣早，也很感動。等到這個部落的最後的與最卑賤的女子加入這一羣粗野而有秩序的人們裏頭的時候，利那披族的男人們圍住安伽斯，如同從前那樣的緘默，嚴肅及不動。

他們擇一個小岡做柯爾拉的葬地，這裏有一叢初長而好看的松樹，成爲一個愁慘而合宜的樹蔭。女子們抬到

93

THE LAST OF THE MOHICANS

and appropriate shade over the spot. On reaching it the girls deposited their burden, and continued for many minutes waiting, with characteristic patience and native timidity, for some evidence that they whose feelings were most concerned were content with the arrangement. At length the scout, who alone understood their habits, said, in their own language:—

"My daughters have done well; the white men thank them."

Satisfied with this testimony in their favor, the girls proceeded to deposit the body in a shell,[1] ingeniously, and not inelegantly, fabricated of the bark of the birch; after which they lowered it into its dark and final abode. The ceremony of covering the remains, and concealing the marks of the fresh earth, by leaves and other natural and customary objects, was conducted with the same simple and silent forms. But when the labors of the kind beings who had performed these sad and friendly offices were so far completed, they hesitated, in a way to show that they knew not how much further they might proceed. It was in this stage of the rites that the scout again addressed them:—

"My young women have done enough," he said. "The spirit of a pale face has no need of food or raiment, their gifts being according to the heaven of their color. I see," he added, glancing an eye at David, who was preparing his book in a manner that indicated in intention to lead the way in sacred song, "that one who better knows the Christian fashions is about to speak."

The females stood modestly aside, and, from having been the principal actors in the scene, they now became the meek

[1] shell 有外槨的內棺.

94

末 了 的 摩 希 干 人

這裏就放下屍架，等候好幾分鐘，表示她們有特殊的忍耐與土人的胆怯，等候其與這件事最有關係的人們表示滿意。只有探子曉得她們的習慣，於是用土話說道：——

『我的女兒們辦得好；白人謝她們。』

這些女子們以這樣的表示為滿意，就進行把遺骸放在一種棺材裏，這個棺材是赤楊樹皮造的，造得也很巧，並不難看；隨後就放入黑暗的穴裏。她們不響的，很單簡的，用土蓋住，用新鮮樹葉及其他天然的及習用的東西，遮掩新土的痕跡。但是等到這些慈心的女子們把這樣悽慘的與表示友誼的事體做到這樣為止時候，她們又遲疑，表示她們不曉得應該怎樣再進行。探子是當殯儀做到這個地步時，又對她們說道：——

『我的少年女人們已經做夠了。白人的精靈，不用食物，不用衣服，她們所贈送的東西是照着她們的種族的神的。』大衛預備好他的書，表示他要領頭唱聖歌，探子看他一眼，說道，『我曉得這個人深知基督教人的風氣，快要說話啦。』

這些女人們謙讓的站在一邊，她們已經做過這件事的主要人物，現在變作婉順的及注意的旁觀人，看隨後的

and attentive observers of that which followed. During the time David was occupied in pouring out the pious feelings of his spirit in this manner, not a sign of surprise, nor a look of impatience, escaped them. They listened like those who knew the meaning of the strange words, and appeared as if they felt the mingled emotions of sorrow, hope, and resignation they were intended to convey.

Excited by the scene he had just witnessed, and perhaps influenced[1] by his own secret emotions, the master of song exceeded his usual efforts. His full rich voice was not found to suffer[2] by a comparison with the soft tones of the girls; and his more modulated strains possessed, at least for the ears of those to whom they were peculiarly addressed, the additional power of intelligence. He ended the anthem, as he had commenced it, in the midst of a grave and solemn stillness.

When, however, the closing cadence had fallen on the ears of his auditors, the secret, timorous glances of the eyes, and the general and yet subdued movement of the assemblage, betrayed that something was expected from the father of the deceased. Munro seemed sensible that the time was come for him to exert what is, perhaps, the greatest effort of which human nature is capable. He bared his gray locks, and looked around the timid and quiet throng by which he was encircled, with a firm and collected countenance. Then motioning with his hand for the scout to listen, he said:—

"Say to these kind and gentle females that a heart-broken and failing man returns them his thanks. Tell them that the Being we all worship, under different names,

---

[1] influenced 潛移. [2] not found to suffer 不見得吃虧.

禮節。當大衛這樣說出他的虔敬感情的時候,那些女子並不流露驚異的或不耐煩的神氣。她們留心聽,好像曉得這些外國話的意思, 好像覺得那些話所欲表示的憂戚, 希望,及聽天由命的夾雜情緒。

這個唱歌先生被他方才所看見的情景所激動, 也許是被他自己的祕密情緒所潛移, 他超過他的向來用慣的氣力。他的豐富聲音同女子們的柔和腔調相比並不吃虧;他的更為悠揚的腔調,是從知性流露出來的,所以加倍有力,原是專對白人唱的,從白人耳朵聽來,至少也是這樣。他起首唱及唱完聖歌的時候,都是在嚴肅與寂靜之中。

但是當結束的尾音落在聽者的耳朵的時候,衆人眼睛所流露的祕密的及畏怯的眼色, 還有羣衆的普通的卻是強制住的行動,表示他們料到死者的父親有點動作。孟洛好像曉得時候到了,他要出盡人類所能做到的力量。他露出他的灰白頭髮, 四面看看包圍他的胆小的及安靜的羣衆,他的神色是堅決而淡定的。他於是舉手請探子留心聽他說話:——

他說道,『請你對這些慈愛而溫和的女人們說,我這個傷心絕望的人謝謝她們。你告訴她們,我們所同拜的上帝,所用的名稱雖然不同,會注意她們的慈善;為日不遠,

will be mindful of their charity; and that the time shall not be distant when we may assemble around the throne without distinction of sex, or rank, or color."

The scout listened to the tremulous voice in which the veteran delivered these words, and shook his head slowly when they were ended, as one who doubted their efficacy.

"To tell them this," he said, "would be to tell them that the snows come not in the winter, or that the sun shines fiercest when the trees are stripped of their leaves."

Then turning to the women, he made such a communication of the other's gratitude as he deemed most suited to the capacities of his listeners. The head of Munro had already sunk upon his chest, and he was again fast relapsing into melancholy, when the young Frenchman before named ventured to touch him lightly on the elbow. As soon as he had gained the attention of the mourning old man, he pointed toward a group of young Indians, who approached with a light but closely covered litter, and then pointed upward toward the sun.

"I understand you, sir," returned Munro, with a voice of forced firmness: "I understand you. It is the will of Heaven, and I submit. Cora, my child! if the prayers of a heart-broken father could avail thee now, how blessed shouldst thou be! Come, gentlemen," he added, looking about him with an air of lofty composure, though the anguish that quivered in his faded countenance was far too powerful to be concealed, "our duty here is ended; let us depart."

Heyward gladly obeyed a summons that took them from a spot where, each instant, he felt his self-control was about to desert him. While his companions were mounting, however, he found time to press the hand of the scout,

將來有一天，我們可以不分男女，不問貴賤，不論白色或黑色，同聚在上帝殿的左右。』

　　探子留心細聽這個老將說話的抖抖聲音，等到說完的時候，他慢慢搖頭，好像不信這樣的說話會有效力。

　　他說道，『告訴她們這樣的話，就是告訴她們雪不是冬天下的，不然就是說當樹葉盡落的時候，太陽光最猛烈。』

　　他於是掉過臉來，對她們說，他把她們以爲最入耳的話說一番，以傳達老將的感謝。孟洛的頭已經垂到胸前，很快又回到憂鬱情景，剛才所說的那個少年法蘭西人輕輕的摸他的肩膀。他一得了這個傷感的老人的注意，他就指着一羣印度少年，他們走近前來，帶着一張輕而遮嚴了的床，他隨即向上指太陽。

　　孟洛勉作堅決聲音，答道，『先生，我明白你的意思，我明白你的意思，這是天意，我服從。柯爾拉，我的孩子呀！倘若一個傷心父親的祈禱現在能夠有益於你，你該多麼受上天所賜的福呀！』 他帶着高超的鎭靜神色四圍一看，說道，『先生們，我們所應盡的本務已經完了，我們走吧。』他的傷痛在他的豐采已退的臉上顫動得利害，他想遮掩也遮掩不來。

　　哈華特願意聽他的吩咐，離開這個地方，他在這裏覺得時時刻刻都把持不住自己。當他的同伴們上馬的時候，他找着時候抓探子的手，重說一遍他們兩人所預定的期

and to repeat the terms of an engagement they had made to meet again within the posts of the British army. Then gladly throwing himself into the saddle, he spurred his charger to the side of the litter, whence low and stifled sobs alone announced the presence of Alice. In this manner, the head of Munro again dropping on his bosom, with Heyward and David following in sorrowing silence, and attended by the aid of Montcalm with his guard, all the white men, with the exception of Hawkeye, passed from before the eyes of the Delawares, and were soon buried in the vast forests of that region.

But the tie which, through their common calamity, had united the feelings of these simple dwellers in the woods with the strangers who had thus transiently visited them, was not so easily broken. Years passed away before the traditionary tale of the white maiden and of the young warrior of the Mohicans ceased to beguile the long nights and tedious marches, or to animate their youthful and brave with a desire for vengeance. Neither were the secondary actors in these momentous incidents forgotten. Through the medium of the scout, who served for years afterward as a link between them and civilized life, they learned, in answer to their inquiries, that the "Grey Head" was speedily gathered to his fathers—borne down, as was erroneously believed, by his military misfortunes; and that the "Open Hand" had conveyed his surviving daughter far into the settlements of the "pale faces," where her tears had at last ceased to flow, and had been succeeded by the bright smiles which were better suited to her joyous nature.

But these were events of a time later than that which concerns our tale. Deserted by all of his color, Hawkeye

末 了 的 摩 希 干 人

約，在不列顛軍隊所駐紮的境內再見。他隨即很高興的跳上馬鞍，用靴距催他的馬快走，走到那架昇床旁邊，只有從床上出來的低聲飲泣，表示在床上的是阿立斯。（孟洛的第二個小姐——譯者註。）孟洛的頭又垂至胸口，哈華特與大衛跟着，滿肚的憂戚，不發一言，還有蒙特卡木（Montcalm 法蘭西軍長——譯者註。）派來幫忙的幾個衛隊，也跟着走，全數的白人（鷹眼除外）就是這樣在狄拉維爾人面前走過，不久，就深入該處的大樹林。

　　但是同經患難所發生的關繫，曾聯絡這些單簡的林居人的感情於暫時來探望他們的外國人，這樣的關繫不是這樣容易就打斷的。歷代相傳下來所說白人的小姐與摩希干的少年戰士的故事，到了夜長寂寞，及路長無聊，或鼓舞少年人及勇敢人報仇雪恥的時候，都要說這段故事，過了許多年，才無人說起。在這幾件重要事體裏頭的幾個次要人物，也是他們所不能忘的。後來有許多年，探子當這些土人及文明國的居間人，做兩族的一個連環，他答復他們的詢問，他們才曉得那個『白頭老人』很快的回去，同他的祖先們相聚——他們誤信他是因爲打敗仗而死的；他們又曉得『肯花錢的人』（殆指哈華特——譯者註。）走遠路送老人的小姐到白人的僑居地，到了那裏，後來就不流涕了，繼以有光彩的微笑，這更宜於她的快樂性情。

　　但是這都是後來的事，在與我們這段故事有相干的事體之後。再說鷹眼當全數白人走過之後，回去他自己的

101

returned to the spot where his own sympathies led him, with a force that no ideal bond of union could bestow. He was just in time to catch a parting look of the features of Uncas, whom the Delawares were already inclosing in his last vestments of skins. They paused to permit the longing and lingering gaze of the sturdy woodsman, and when it was ended, the body was enveloped, never to be unclosed again. Then came a procession like the other, and the whole nation was collected about the temporary grave of the chief—temporary, because it was proper that, at some future day, his bones should rest among those of his own people.

The movement, like the feeling, had been simultaneous[1] and general. The same grave expression of grief, the same rigid silence, and the same deference to the principal mourner were observed around the place of interment as have already been described. The body was deposited in an attitude of repose, facing the rising sun, with the implements of war and of the chase close at hand, in readiness for the final journey. An opening was left in the shell, by which it was protected from the soil, for the spirit to communicate with its earthly tenement, when necessary; and the whole was concealed from the instinct, and protected from the ravages of the beasts of prey, with an ingenuity peculiar to the natives. The manual rites then ceased, and all present reverted to the more spiritual part of the ceremonies.

Chingachgook became once more the object of the common attention. He had not yet spoken, and something consolatory and instructive was expected from so renowned

---

[1] simultaneous 同 時 的; 出 于 自 然 的.

末 了 的 摩 希 干 人

哀憐所引他去的地點，這樣的吸力，無論是什麼理想的契合所不能給的。他剛好及時見安伽斯一面，與他永遠分手，那時候狄拉維爾人正在用最後幾層皮革裹他的屍。他們停手一會兒，讓這個壯健的獵人很捨不得的多看死者一會，等他看完了，就把屍首裹嚴了，永遠再不打開的了。隨後就是排班送殯，同送柯爾拉的一樣，全個民族都聚在這個酋長的臨時葬地——這不過是臨時的，因爲將來有一天，總要把他的骸骨葬在他自己人們的墳地。

他們的舉動，同他們的感情一樣，都是出於自然的，又是人人都有的。他們在葬地上流露憂戚，謹嚴的緘默，敬禮喪主，同前文所敍的一樣。屍身作休息狀態，面向初出的太陽，打仗與打獵的兵器擺在身邊，預備走最後的路程。棺上留一小洞，棺所以保護屍身，不爲土所侵害，小洞所以使死者的神靈，遇有必要時，可以同地上的住所通往來；掩埋全棺，不使野獸看見，且保護屍身，不被野獸所糟塌，土人有特別巧妙法子保護。手作的葬禮已畢，全數在場的人再行其更屬於精神上的禮節。

慶伽谷又變作衆人所同注意的目的物。他還未曾說話，他原是一個有名的酋長，又當舉行這樣有意味的大典

a chief on an occasion of such interest. Conscious of the wishes of the people, the stern and self-restrained warrior raised his face, which had latterly been buried in his robe, and looked about him with a steady eye. His firmly compressed and expressive lips then severed, and for the first time during the long ceremonies his voice was distinctly audible.

"Why do my brothers mourn?" he said, regarding the dark race of dejected warriors by whom he was environed. "Why do my daughters weep? That a young man has gone to the happy hunting grounds; that a chief has filled his time with honor? He was good; he was dutiful; he was brave. Who can deny it? The Manitou had need of such a warrior, and He has called him away. As for me, the son and the father of Uncas, I am a blazed pine, in a clearing of pale faces. My race has gone from the shores of the salt lake and the hills of the Delawares. But who can say that the serpent of his tribe has forgotten his wisdom? I am alone—"

"No, no," cried Hawkeye, who had been gazing with a yearning look at the rigid features of his friend, with something like his own self-command, but whose philosophy could endure no longer; "no, Sagamore, not alone. The gifts of our colors may be different, but God has so placed us as to journey in the same path. I have no kin, and I may also say, like you, no people. He was your son, and a red-skin by nature; and it may be that your blood was nearer—but if ever I forget the lad who has so often fou't[1] at my side in war, and slept at my side in peace, may He who made us all whatever may be our color or our gifts,

---

[1] fou't 即是 fought.

末 了 的 摩 希 干 人

的時機，他們都望他說幾句安慰話，說幾句示訓的話。這個嚴厲而能自制的戰士曉得他們的想望，他本來垂頭埋在他的袍子裏的，這時候抬起頭來，定睛四圍一看。於是分開他的謹閉而有表示的兩唇，當這次行禮行得很久的時候，這是第一次衆人聽見他的清楚聲音。

他看看包圍他的垂頭喪氣的黑種；說道，『我的弟兄們爲什麼悲哀？我的女兒們爲什麼哭？你們悲痛，爲的是一個少年已經往歡樂的園場去麼？爲的是一個酋長不虛生一世已經做了體面的事麼？他是個好人；他是個孝子；他是個勇敢人。誰能不承認呀？曼尼圖要這樣的一個戰士；他宣召他去了。至於我呢，安伽斯的兒子及父親，我是在白人的斬除了草木的園地中的一棵剝了皮作標識的松樹。我的族類已經從鹹水湖的湖濱及狄拉維爾山走開了。但是誰能說他的部落的蛇已經忘記了他的明智？我是孤零——』

鷹眼那時候正在依依不捨看着他朋友的強固不動的面目，帶着多少他自己的自制，但是他的哲學不復能忍得下去，說道，『酋長，不是的，不是的，你並不孤零。上帝雖然賦我們以不同的皮色，但是上帝曾布置我們，使我們同走一條路。我無親屬，我同你一樣，也可以說，我無部民。他是你的兒子，生來就是紅皮膚；以血統論，你們父子兩人可以說是較親——但是這個少年屢次在我的身邊打仗，不打仗的時候常時睡在我身邊，倘若我忘記他，請創造全數人類的上帝也忘記了我！人類不問什麼皮色，亦不

forget me! The boy has left us for a time; but Sagamore, you are not alone."

Chingachgook grasped the hand that, in the warmth of feeling, the scout had stretched across the fresh earth, and in that attitude of friendship these two sturdy and intrepid woodsmen bowed their heads together, while scalding tears fell to their feet, watering the grave of Uncas like drops of falling rain.

In the midst of the awful stillness with which such a burst of feeling, coming, as it did, from the two most renowned warriors of that region, was received, Tamenund lifted his voice to disperse the multitude.

"It is enough," he said. "Go, children of the Lenape, the anger of the Manitou is not done. Why should Tamenund stay? The pale faces are masters of the earth, and the time of the red men has not yet come again. My day has been too long. In the morning I saw the sons of Unamis happy and strong; and yet, before the night has come, have I lived to see the last warrior of the wise race of the Mohicans."

末　了　的　摩　希　干　人

問賢愚，全是上帝造的。這個孩子不過暫時離開我們；酋長，你卻並不孤零。』

探子發表他的感情發得熱烈，在新掘的土上伸手過去，慶伽谷抓住這隻手，這兩個剛健無畏的獵人做了朋友，同時點首，兩個人的熱淚滴在脚下，淚落如雨，灑安伽斯的墳。

衆人看見這個地方的兩個最有名的戰士湧出這樣熱烈的感情，正在蕭然敬畏，靜寂無聲，塔米能說話，遣散衆人。

他說道，『夠了。利那披的孩子們，走吧，曼尼圖的怒氣未消。塔米能爲什麼逗留？白人是世界的主人翁，紅人的時機還未再來。我的日子太長了。我在早上看見烏那米斯 (Unamis) 的子孫歡樂壯健；但是天還未黑，我活到這個時候，反看見摩希干的明智種族的末了一個戰士。』

書名：末了的摩希干人（英漢對照）
系列：漢英對照經典英文文學文庫
主編：潘國森、陳劍聰
原作者:庫柏
漢譯:伍光健

出版：心一堂有限公司
地址：香港九龍旺角彌敦道610號
　　　荷李活商業中心18樓1805-06室
電話號碼：(852) 6715-0840
網址：www.sunyata.cc
　　　publish.sunyata.cc
電郵：sunyatabook@gmail.com
心一堂讀者論壇：http://bbs.sunyata.cc
網上書店：http://book.sunyata.cc

香港發行：香港聯合書刊物流有限公司
香港新界大埔汀麗路36號中華商務印刷
大廈3樓
電話號碼：(852)2150-2100
傳真號碼：(852)2407-3062
電郵：info@suplogistics.com.hk

台灣發行：秀威資訊科技股份有限公司
地址：台灣台北市內湖區瑞光路七十六巷
　　　六十五號一樓
電話號碼：+886-2-2796-3638
傳真號碼：+886-2-2796-1377
網絡書店：www.bodbooks.com.tw
心一堂台灣國家書店讀者服務中心：
地址：台灣台北市中山區松江路二0九號1樓
電話號碼：+886-2-2518-0207
傳真號碼：+886-2-2518-0778
網址：www.govbooks.com.tw

中國大陸發行 零售：
　　　　　深圳心一堂文化传播有限公司
深圳：中國深圳羅湖立新路六號東門
　　　博雅負一層零零八號
電話號碼：(86)0755-82224934
北京：中國北京東城區雍和宮大街四十號
心一堂官方淘寶流通處：
http://sunyatacc.taobao.com/

版次：2019年4月初版

　　　HKD 88
定價：NT　348

國際書號　978-988-8582-60-0

版權所有　翻印必究

Title: The Last of the Mohicans
 (with Chinese translation)
Series: Classic English Literature
Collections with Chinese Translation
Editor: POON, Kwok-Sum(MCIoL,
DipTranCIoL), CHEN, Kim
by James Fenimore Coope
Translated and Annotated (in Chinese)
by Woo Kwang-Kien

Published in Hong Kong by Sunyata Ltd
Address: Unit 1805-06, 18/F, Hollywood Plaza,610
Nathan Road, Mong Kok, Kowloon, Hong Kong
Tel: (852) 6715-0840
Website: publish.sunyata.cc
Email: sunyatabook@fmail.com
Online bookstore: http://book.sunyata.cc

Distributed in Hong Kong by:
SUP PUBLISHING LOGISTICS(HK)
LIMITED
Address：3/F, C & C Buliding,
36 Ting Lai Road, Tai Po, N.T.,
Hong Kong
Tel：(852) 2150-2100
Fax：(852) 2407-3062
E-mail：info@suplogistics.com.hk

Distributed in Taiwan by:
Showwe Information Co. Ltd.
Address: 1/F, No.65, Lane 76, Rueiguang
Road, Neihu District, Taipei, Taiwan
Website: www.bodbooks.com.tw

First Edition April 2019
HKD 88
NT 348

ISBN: 978-988-8582-60-0

All rights reserved.